To Willow.

Best wishes

Shane Robinson

THE
AMAZING
FARTZINI

An incredible story about an

incredible boy who found magic!

SHANE ROBINSON

Other books by the author:

The Amazing Fartzini II: The magical
adventures of a boy wizard continue …

The Amazing Fartzini III: Finale

ISBN: 978-1-9162356-1-8

DEDICATION

I dedicate this book to all the 'Dreamers' out there! Because, without 'Dreamers', you'd be reading this book on a stone tablet, and living in a cold and damp cave! Or possibly the human race would have become extinct a long, long time ago – and then would've definitely had no chance of reading this book!

INTRODUCTION
By the Author

In case you are wondering whether this book you now have in your possession is a 'Fictional Storybook', a 'Magic Book', or a 'Self-help Book'? Well, it's all three! You see I didn't just want to write yet another 'Beginners Magic Book' explaining just tricks! I hope this book will be inspiring and enable the young reader not only to learn the magic tricks taught but more importantly how to become self-confident, admired and respected through performing magic – as well as enjoying the story of course!

So, at its core, the book is about helping children to believe in themselves and be confident. And I thought if I write a story this will help to get my advice across to children in perhaps a better, more effective way!

It is a fictional story about a schoolboy called Eric Fartz, who lacks self-confidence and is bullied. But, by a chance meeting at the local Christmas Fair with a wise old magician, decides to take up performing magic, which he finds really helps him to gain confidence and eventually turn his life around for the better!

However, this story could've just as easily been written about many young people struggling with confidence issues in the real world today. Maybe that's you? If so, then this book will be most helpful to you.

Throughout the story, Eric amazes everyone with his cool magic tricks, and a lot of these tricks are taught in 'Eric's Magic Trick Secrets' at the rear of the book – so you too will be able to amaze people like Eric!

All the magic tricks taught in this book I have carefully chosen with the beginner to magic in mind. I wanted to choose the type of magic tricks that are simple and easy enough to learn, but yet effective, and that you could perform on the spur of the moment using everyday objects that you can easily find around you. Some of these tricks you will find more challenging to learn than others, but it is always good to stretch yourself so you can improve!

I have explained all the magic tricks taught how I accomplish them, which include many of my own additional idea's. They are all magic tricks I still perform myself to this day, so I can certainly vouch for their effectiveness. Some of them date back hundreds of years, whilst some are more recent. And, I couldn't write a book teaching magic tricks without including one I created myself, called 'Lucky Thirteen'.

Also included towards the rear of the magic book section is a 'Glossary', which you will find very useful for learning and understanding the various magic related terms used.

I have been a professional magician for many years and my stage name is called 'Zane'. I am also the owner of a well-established and respected magic shop business in the UK called 'Zane's Magic Shop'. So, I am very qualified to write this book. And the advice and motivation I give to you in these pages come from many years' experience and trial and error.

One of the things you learn from performing magic for as long as I have, is human psychology and behavior. So, you will also find in amongst the story, written in italics, advice on not only performing magic but how to become, if need be, more outgoing and confident, and how to deal with bullying.

I receive a lot of lovely comments from parents, thanking me for inspiring their children, and here is an email I received recently from an acquaintance of mine I thought would be good to include as proof of the power of performing magic:

"Hi Zane,

I was performing magic for some guests in a restaurant,

and they told me a nice story.

They live in Dartford and were at a nearby event, and there was a magician with a stall. Their child, around 10 years old, wasn't really interested, in fact, was not really interested in anything apart from computer games.

Anyway, they dragged the child over to the magician's stand, and within minutes he was transfixed, watching the magician perform, demonstrating tricks.

They bought quite a few tricks, and the child has spent months practising them, wanting to do them as well as the magician. He has practically given up computer games, and spends hours practising card tricks, and has even invented a few of his own.

"That magician," they told me, "changed our son's life. He was just inspirational!"

I had to ask.

"That's wonderful, what was his name?"

"Zane!"

Thought you would like to know, selling tricks is special work indeed! ..."

It's always nice and rewarding for me to hear about real life stories like this! Testimony to this is how much magic has helped me in life, especially as a child growing up!

Well, I very much hope you enjoy reading my book and learning the cool and amazing magic tricks and have as much fun performing them as I have over the years!

CHAPTER ONE

THE BULLYING HAS STARTED!

Eric Fartz, an eleven-year-old schoolboy, was being forcibly pinned up against his school locker again by two school bullies from the year above! "Give us your dinner money or else!" said David, aggressively. He was a large and overweight big mouth, and the ringleader.

The other even fatter boy, whose nickname was 'Hamburger' because he was always eating them, leaned down even closer towards Eric. "You heard him, *Stinky Farts!*" said 'Hamburger' in his annoyingly high-pitched squeaky voice. His breath stank and Eric could feel his long black greasy hair brushing against his face. The big bully then held up his large chubby clenched fist, threatening to punch the poor boy hard if he didn't pay up!

"Okay! I have it, I have it!" squealed Eric, scared and desperately fighting back the tears. He didn't want to show them he was frightened anymore, but was a weakly boy, short in height for his years and was smart enough to realise he would come out worse, a lot worse if he tried to fight them – they were about twice his size! So, like on most days, he handed over his dinner money to these two horrible boys and went hungry.

It was only recently that Eric joined St. Bartholomew's C of E Comprehensive School in Ramsgate, Kent. Three weeks ago, to be precise, midway through the second term of year seven. He came down with his mum Ingrid from Sheffield – an industrial city in the north of England, where he was born – to start a new life. They had to leave and relocate due to domestic abuse.

His dad Peter was a gambler and had a drinking problem, and would sometimes become violent. One time the police even had to be involved. She had all the locks to the house changed and the courts served him an injunction order to stay away from them, but that didn't seem to work as he would often turn up at the family home drunk, shouting abuse and demanding to come in. One time smashing a window to try to gain access. Enough was enough and Ingrid knew that she and her son had to leave for their own safety.

So, they did, and ended up in Ramsgate. No one's heard of Ramsgate, a small, quiet and remote fishing town on the East Kent coast! His mother who was originally from Germany had heard of it: she was brought over to England on a family trip from Germany via the port of Ramsgate as a teenager. There used to be a ferry crossing from Calais in France to the port of Ramsgate back then. It was on this trip to the north of England where she had a holiday romance with her now estranged partner. And, a few years later lived with him in Sheffield and fell pregnant, given birth to their only child, Eric. They were never actually married, and since she no longer wanted to use his surname – she kept her maiden name Fartz – much to the displeasure of poor little Eric.

Ingrid and her son gave up a lot to move down to Ramsgate. As, although they were by no means well off, they did live reasonably comfortably in a three-bedroom semi-detached house. They also had a nice car, and always had a family summer holiday by the seaside once a year – usually to Scarborough.

So, they both had to make a personal sacrifice. However, it was a lot better they thought, to be in living in Ramsgate without the luxuries, than living in fear as they did back in Sheffield – although for poor little Eric, fear was very much still with him!

Having the surname, Fartz, of course, didn't help with the bullying. Apart from being ridiculed for being short, he often had to endure children making disgusting fart noises and chanting, "Eric farts! Eric farts!" whilst holding their noses, very cruelly taunting him. How Eric wished his mum and dad had got married: then his surname would have been 'Richardson' and he wouldn't have had to put up with all the horrible name calling. He knew the old saying: 'Sticks and stones may break my bones, but names will never hurt me.' But it did hurt Eric's feelings.

Eric would tell people his name was spelt with a 'Z' and not with an 'S', but it didn't make any difference, and after a while he gave up trying to explain it.

Eric hadn't told his mum about the recent bullying at school because he didn't want to worry her further, especially with everything they had been through in Sheffield. Eric was a quiet lad but had a great sense of humour and a vivid imagination. He was short and rather skinny. He hadn't had a growth spurt yet like most of the other children in his class seemed to have had. He had blue eyes and must have been the fairest haired boy in Ramsgate, which no doubt he got from his mum. Although, his mum had since dyed her lovely natural long blonde hair, black, to be incognito. Just like his mum, Eric was kind and considerate and despite being bullied, often had a smile on his face. He had a great smile! He was a happy, go lucky type of boy.

"Hi, Mum. I'm home, what's for tea?" Eric called out as he opened the back door into the kitchen.

"Never mind that," said his mum. "What's that mud doing on your face again?"

"It's one of your face packs Mum," quipped Eric. Eric could be very witty at times.

"*Look* at your face!" his mum said, slightly concerned.

"I fell over playing football," he replied convincingly. Eric liked football and was a keen Sheffield United supporter – although, he wasn't very good at playing it. His dad used to take him to Bramall Lane to watch 'The Blades' play whenever the team were at home. "Sheff United!" and "Come on you Blades!" he used to enjoy chanting with his dad in the terraces.

There were three things he really missed

living in the South of England: watching his favourite team play football, walking in the beautiful Derbyshire countryside and 'Mushy Peas'!

"Okay, well go and wash yourself and your tea will be ready by the time you've finished," said his mum, frowning.

Actually, he told his mum a fib. He had his face pushed into some muddy grass by the two bullies on the way home from school!

"Eat grass!" said David mockingly; laughing as he pushed Eric's face into the muddy grass, while 15 stone 'Hamburger' held him down by sitting on him.

"Hurry up David – I'm hungry!" squeaked 'Hamburger', thinking of his stomach as usual. His voice hadn't broken yet, and it sounded comical to hear a high-pitched squeaky voice coming out of the mouth of such a large boy.

"Don't you dare grass on us, northerner!" said David threateningly. "Grass! D'ya get it Hamburger?" Both bullies laughed out loud in unison at this unintended pun, like a pair of hyenas. They thought it was hilarious, but it wasn't at all funny for Eric!

Both the bullies were immature for their age, especially 'Hamburger'. But at least the laughter distracted them and saved poor little Eric from further intimidation, as they then decided to leave him alone, and carried on their way home. Eric could still hear them laughing their heads off in the distance.

Eric was becoming a good liar. He was certainly getting enough practice at it. But only because he didn't want to admit that he was being bullied!

"Here you are love. Make sure you eat up all your tea!" said his mum as she put his meal on the table. His mum had cooked him his favourite meal. A traditional German dish, called 'Bratkartoffeln'. Basically, fried potatoes with diced fatty bacon, onions, and a fried egg on top.

Eric was starving by now and left nothing on the plate. He probably would have eaten the plate as well if it were edible. Although he was missing his lunches, his mum always made sure he went to school with a good bowl of porridge or muesli and a piece of fruit – usually a banana as he didn't like most other fruits – and always had a hearty meal at teatime. One meal he hated but got given several times a week was beans on toast. It wasn't that he didn't like the taste of baked beans: it was because he was always worried that after eating them, he would live up to the horrid names his tormentors called him called. Luckily though, he didn't get baked beans for breakfast before going to school.

His mum was now bringing Eric up on her own as a single parent, living on a council estate in a very, basic, tiny ground floor flat, and she no longer had monetary support from her ex-partner. Their new address was number 76a, Hope Close, which the road sign now read as: 'No Hope Close', no thanks to a local graffiti artist with a cynical sense of humour.

So, times were hard, and it really felt like there was no hope for them at times. But she was determined not to let the current situation drag them down and got by the best she could. Sometimes though, she struggled to make ends meet and would have to miss meals herself to ensure Eric always had a good meal on the table each day. Sometimes it was the harsh decision of either keeping warm or eating. It was wintertime, and sometimes it was very, cold in their council flat because she couldn't always afford to pay the meter. Poor little Eric often missed out on treats that most kids in the area enjoyed and took for granted. This upset her more than anything.

Ingrid managed to get part-time work during the week at a local supermarket working at the checkout, which helped with the bills. Her English was very good, having lived in the UK for many years, but she still had an accent. It was a cross between a German and northern English accent, which she hated and often felt self-conscious of it. Ingrid had already made a few friends from work, and this really helped lift her spirits.

Eric, on the other hand, was struggling to make friends. He was becoming more inward than ever before and would often shut himself in his room and be self-absorbed playing one video game after another, which quietly started to worry his mum. He was a bright lad and had always done well at school, so his mum didn't worry too much about him playing video games on his old 'PlayStation', which he got as Christmas present when times were a lot better. Besides, it kept him out of mischief she concluded.

After finishing his dinner and doing the washing up, just like clockwork, Eric went and shut himself in his room. But unlike most days, this time he didn't immediately pick up his 'PlayStation' controls; he sat quietly on the edge of his bed thinking about the ordeal he had endured that day because of those two bullies, and that he could not let this carry on anymore. Especially stealing from him – he knew how hard his mum had worked for that money.

The trouble was he had no idea how he was

going to deal with it. He thought if he told his mum and it was reported to the school, it would only make things worse for him. Also, his mum seemed to be on the up, and even perhaps happy once again. It had been a while! He could always tell because his mum started singing again when she cooked his food. She always did that when she was happy. She didn't make anyone else happy with her singing though. She had a dreadful voice, especially singing in English with a thick German accent. Even their cat, they used to have in Sheffield would dart through the cat flap the moment she started to sing. Just for fun, Eric and his dad would cringe and put their fingers in their ears, and the three of them would laugh about it together.

"If only she didn't attempt to hit the high notes! And, if only I had one of those buzzers like on The X Factor!" thought Eric. A grin, then a smile cracked on his face as he remembered a happier time in Sheffield before his dad started drinking heavily and the problems began.

Anyway, for now, he'd forgotten about the bullies and with an almost involuntary flick on the remote, on came his T.V monitor, and he was playing a game of 'FIFA'. "GOAL" he shouted. His team was Sheffield United of course, and they were one-nil up!

Later that evening, his mum came to tuck him in and kiss him goodnight, but he'd fallen asleep playing his video games. She noticed a piece of paper by his bedside with just the heading: 'Plan', and the capital letter: 'D', written on the next line. The rest of the paper was blank?

CHAPTER TWO

DOWN IN THE DUMPS

The next morning Eric awoke, feeling as if his eyelids had been super-glued shut. The 'Sandman' had been again in the night. Though, his dreams were far from pleasant: since the bullying started, Eric would often wake up in the middle of the night sobbing from having ghastly nightmares. Indeed, Eric rarely woke up to a dry pillow.

Eric wiped away the crust from his dried tears and quickly got ready for school – as he daren't be late again. He would have much preferred to stay in bed all day if he could! He quickly gulped down half a slice of toast, put on his grey school blazer, followed by his grey duffle coat, opened the front door and stepped outside into the grey and dreary weather. "Tarra Mum!" he called out as he slammed the door behind him and hurriedly dashed off to his new school in Ramsgate.

"Tarra love!" she called back. She often called him 'Love'. A term she picked up living in the north. Eric put on a brave face, but really, he was dreading going to school because he knew it was likely to be another day of him being bullied.

The trouble with being repeatedly bullied is that it seems like it will never end for the victim. Eric didn't have any social media accounts like 'Facebook' or 'Instagram', as a lot of his fellow school pupils had. So at least the bullies couldn't bully him on social media platforms as well, which no doubt they would have done. His mum didn't allow it for the time being at least, because she was worried that her ex might find out where they are now living. *(The best way to deal with 'Cyber Bullying' is to not respond to the bullies directly. Report the abuse immediately to your parents or guardians, and the authorities if need be. And ban them from your social media platforms. Don't allow yourself to be affected by it and drawn into communicating with them. It will only cause it to escalate, which is what the bullies want!)*

To get to school, Eric first had to walk out of

the estate, and then either walk about 300 metres along the main road, past the row of local shops, cross the busy road, then wind his way along a few smaller roads before arriving at the gates of his new school. Or, save himself a lot of time and risk cutting across the same playing fields where he got his face pushed into the muddy ground the day before.

Well, since Eric was not very good at getting up in the mornings, the latter option was very appealing to him. So, against his better judgement, he decided to take the more precarious shortcut again across the playing fields to school.

He walked briskly across the lonely field on this cold and cloudy day, thinking, "Where are they?" He had just passed the children's play area, which consisted of just broken swings, a rusty old slide and roundabout, and where the two bullies often liked to hang out. They would often play truant, drink high energy drinks and smoke cigarettes before mums with pushchairs would arrive and tell them to clear off. But there was still no sign of them anywhere. "Strange!" Eric thought, and carried on walking. Then suddenly, he heard a loud scream.

"THERE HE IS – GET 'IM!" one of the two bullies called out as they began to chase after him. They had arrived later than usual that morning, coming across the field from a different direction.

Eric thought, "I wish I had one of those 'Invisibility Cloaks', like in the Harry Potter books!" Although, to some extent, Eric was invisible to most other people, because he was so quiet and unnoticeable. Except to bullies, of course, who tend to pick on the quiet ones. Thankfully for Eric, they were both very overweight and couldn't run very fast.

"Oi, come here you northerner!" one of them screeched. But Eric had already left the starting blocks, running faster than he'd ever run before. Even Usain Bolt would have struggled to keep up with him. He was at least twenty metres ahead of them and could now see the school in front of him.

Eric turned his head around as he ran and retaliated from a distance, shouting back, "Catch me if you can – you, *southern* wusses!" The other boys gave up the chase realising it was a waste of time, panting heavily as they now walked. Eric's heart was racing so much, it felt like it was about to burst out of his chest!

"We'll get you later … *Northern* Monkey!" David called out angrily.

"Thank God for that!" Eric thought as he entered the school gates after his routine daily morning exercise. He then went straight to his classroom. "Now all I've got to do," he thought, "is to avoid them all day!"

"Your earlier than usual Fartz?" said his form tutor Mr Potter, peering over the rim of his glasses at him. "What's the matter with you, are you feeling alright?" continued Mr Potter with a dry sense of humour to lots of giggles as Eric entered the classroom, still panting. Mr Potter, who was getting on in years and soon due for retirement, was a real character.

"Morning sir," said Eric as he headed quickly for his desk at the back of the class with his shirt hanging out and looking rather sweaty. As he sat down, he just caught a glimpse through the classroom door window of the two bullies passing by. One looked menacingly into the classroom as if searching for him.

"Right, settle down and be quiet!" yelled the teacher. "It's come to my attention that not all of you have handed in your history homework, and therefore the following pupils will have detention tonight. Barker, Robinson, Williamson – and, oh, *what* a surprise ...! *Fartz!*" Some of the kids in the class giggled again. "Silence ...! Well, what have you got to say for yourselves?" There was a long silence. "This is not the first time you haven't handed in your homework, is it Fartz? What's your excuse this time? Don't tell me your *dog* ate it again!" Mr Potter stroked his goatee beard, trying to calm himself down.

"Well ... no sir, my dog didn't eat it ... but my neighbour's dog did!" replied Eric nervously. The class howled with laughter. Quietly, Eric enjoyed this newfound attention.

"Class, I said be QUIET!" shouted the teacher again, throwing the formbook down onto table with a loud bang as he said the word 'quiet'. "No excuses Fartz! I will see you in detention after school tonight!"

"Why? Did you do something wrong as well sir?" one of the naughty pupils at the back quipped to more giggles around the class.

"*Right!* Who said that? Was it you Robinson? *Right!* Have another detention!"

The classroom went quiet, but then all of a sudden, a loud rip-roaring fart sound was heard. Somebody had purposely got up from their seat and plonked themselves back down onto a 'Whoopee Cushion' making a horrendous sound, followed by an uproar of laughter.

"*Right!* Who did that?" demanded the teacher, now starting to boil over with anger.

"It was *Fartz*, sir!" claimed the naughty prankster pointing at poor Eric. More laughter was heard as the teacher struggled to control his unruly class. "No, it wasn't sir – honest!" protested Eric, embarrassed that the whole class were staring at him, laughing and giggling, some holding their noses.

"There's only one thing for it," thought, Mr Potter "To use my "Trump Card'!" Finding it hard to keep a straight face and not burst out laughing at his unintentional word choice. So, in a last-ditch attempt to maintain order in his class, Mr Potter shook his forefinger in the air and yelled, "Whoever the culprit was, bring that 'Whoopee Cushion' to me *now!* Or ... the *whole* class will have detention!" not fooled for one minute as to what made the fart-like sound.

Well, it must have worked because the giggling stopped and the classroom fell silent as they all turned their gaze and pointed towards the now red-faced guilty individual, who promptly brought the soggy 'Whoopee Cushion' up to the front of the class.

"Sorry, sir!" said the boy nervously as he handed it over to the teacher.

"Consider this confiscated – and you can join the other lot in detention! Now go and *sit* down!" sternly said Mr Potter as he gingerly dropped the 'Whoopee Cushion' into his desk drawer. The thought of pranking the other teachers in the staff room entering his mind.

Mr Potter then opened the register and began calling out pupil's names ...

As Eric was leaving the classroom on his way to his first lesson of the day, Mr Potter remarked, "You don't seem that bothered you've got detention young man?" And he wasn't. Eric had purposely not given his homework in, even though he had done it. He knew that by not doing so he would be given a detention and it would mean the bullies couldn't set upon him after school – at least for today. Given him more time to work out his plan.

Well, the day went by and Eric managed to avoid the bullies, sometimes hiding from them as they walked past. He also stopped using his locker where he knew they would sometimes wait for him, and with some difficulty lugged his heavy bag of schoolbooks around with him all day.

There was one close shave though. Eric was in the Boys Toilets just having a pee in one of the cubicles during one of the breaks – he would often go in the cubicles rather than use the urinals, fearing the bullies might walk in. Well, luckily, he locked the door behind him, as on this occasion, David and his cohort 'Hamburger' did walk in. Eric could recognize their voices anywhere! He immediately froze in a state of terror, accidentally peeing down his trousers.

Eric could overhear them just opposite him at the urinals chatting. "We'll wait for him by the school gates again," said David. Eric knew exactly who he meant by 'him'. He kept as quiet as he possibly could, waiting for them to leave, before he dared to open the door. *Finally,* they left, and he quietly undid the lock and freed himself from the cubicle, relieved that the bullies had gone. He quickly wiped the groin area of his trousers with a wet paper towel, making it look much worse than before, and then made his way to the classroom, strategically covering the enormous wet patch with his school bag as he did, feeling very self-conscious. Eric didn't think the bullies would wait around for him after detention, as he knew they liked their food so much and would want to get home to eat their tea. Of course, he would now have the problem of explaining to his mum why he got detention, as the school would have phoned the parents to inform them.

For a change, he came in through the flat door with a smile on his face having outwitted the bullies. That smile soon dropped though as his mum, who was now the disciplinarian told him off for not doing his homework and for telling lies about the dog they never had. As a punishment, he had his 'PlayStation' confiscated and was banned from playing video games for one week. But even worse, he had beans on toast again for tea that night. His mum tried to find out if there was anything wrong but got no answers.

"So that strategy isn't going to work anymore," Eric thought to himself. Eric made sure he got all his homework done and later that evening in his room tried to plan out his next approach to tackling the bullies. He knew they would be even angrier with him now he had evaded giving them his dinner money, and who knows what they might do to him now! But nothing came to him and his mind was as blank as the paper in front of him. It was late and Eric was now feeling tired and gave up trying.

"Eric! Would you like a nice cup of hot chocolate?" called out his mum from the kitchen. His mum normally made him a cup of hot chocolate before bedtime.

"Yes, please Mum!" replied Eric as he was getting into his 'Marvel Comic' pyjamas, whilst at the same time trying to insert a DVD into the DVD player to watch his favourite movie 'Superman' in bed.

"Okay, I'll put the kettle on love," then called

out his mum.

Eric woke up early the next morning in a sweat: he'd been having a nightmare, dreaming the two bullies were dangling him upside down out of an upstairs classroom window so his dinner money would fall out of his pockets, laughing their heads off. His form teacher Mr Potter was there also, repeatedly shouting, "Detention!" while steam bizarrely came pouring out of his ears as if he was about to blow his top like a boiling kettle.

"It's only a dream! It's only a dream!" he kept telling himself. Though, he wouldn't put anything past those two horrible boys. Suddenly he thought, "I know! I'll throw a 'Sicky', then I won't have to go to school!" but then he thought, "No, that won't work with my mum — she's much too clever to believe that — and then she'll know something's up!" Then after some deliberation, he thought, "I know! I'll break open my piggy bank and offer the bullies what I have saved if they will leave him alone!" He was desperate now.

He discovered that he had £22.47 in total left. Most of the money he'd already spent buying second-hand video games from a video games store in Sheffield before he left. Twenty pounds of it was from his nan and grandpa in Germany, intended for him to buy a present with it! "I will offer them twenty pounds — that's ten pounds each, and then I won't have to hand over Mums hard earned money anymore!" he naively thought. *(This was a big mistake, and Eric would soon learn the hard way, as you should NEVER hand money over to bullies because it shows a sign of weakness. And then the bullies will just keep coming back for more! You can't negotiate or reason with bullies because they often get a thrill out of it and like to be controlling. It's a power thing!)*

So off Eric went to school, taking the shortcut again with two crumpled ten-pound notes in his pocket. This time the two bullies were waiting for him, sat on the broken swings, looking angry and calling out abuse as he approached them.

"What's that horrible smell? Hold your nose here comes *'Stinky Fartz'!*" cruelly said 'Hamburger'.

"You're *dead!*" called out David sinisterly. As soon as Eric heard this, he nervously removed the cash from his pocket, holding it up in front of him, his hand visibly shaking with the look of fear and dread etched on his face!

The two boys were expecting a chase again, but Eric bravely held his nerve and kept heading towards them. David flicked the cigarette away he'd been smoking, coughing a couple of times, and said, "Oh, look 'Hamburger', Christmas must have come early!"

David promptly walked over to the very scared younger boy and snatched the money out of his hand. "*I'll* take that," he said and pushed him against his chest, which hurt.

"You can have it, just please leave me alone from now on!" Eric pleaded with them.

David mockingly repeated what Eric had said in a poor northern accent. "*Please leave me alone. Leave* you alone! *Leave* you alone!" responded David in an intimidating way. "I'll tell you when we'll leave you alone ... I know, let's give him a ride on the roundabout!" said David menacingly. 'Hamburger' then squeezed himself out of the swing seat to join his partner in crime. Both grabbed hold of one arm each and dragged the now screaming boy in the direction of the roundabout.

"No, no, leave me alone!" Eric pleaded once more, trembling with fear. Now only slightly struggling, realising the inevitable. As sure enough, Eric's screams fell on deaf ears as the two bullies chucked him on the roundabout and started spinning it as fast as they could. Faster and faster it went. It was too dangerous now to try to jump off. So, Eric crouched down holding on for dear life, feeling dizzier and dizzier, wishing his punishment would stop.

"Enjoy the ride!" called out David. The two boys thought it was hilarious and kept laughing and spinning it and spinning it. "Get me off … pleeeease!" shrieked Eric, starting to cry.

"Why don't you learn to speak proper English, you, *northern* cry baby?" said David.

"Yeah! Why don't you learn to speak proper English, you, *northern* crybaby?" repeated 'Hamburger', much to David's annoyance. He would often repeat what David had said. He then exclaimed in his usual immature way, "Oh yeah, and you wouldn't have run faster than us if it was a proper race!"

"Yeah, that's right, you, *skanky* Northern Monkey!" then called out David in agreement.

An old man walking their dog had heard the screams and spotted what was going on. *"Hey, you leave that boy alone!"* shouted the passer-by in aid of the poor defenceless boy. His dog then started barking loudly. Upon hearing this, the two bullyboys made a run for it, leaving the roundabout still spinning.

"Let's go!" said the ringleader David. Both the unruly boys now directing their abuse towards the passer-by as they ran – with a torrent of strong swear words unashamedly rolling off their tongues with well-practised ease – being rude and disrespectful. "This isn't over, Fartz!" then called out David.

Shaken up and bedraggled, Eric still managed to get to school. As he entered his classroom, with his shirt half hanging out again and slightly late, Mr Potter addressed him.

"Mr Fartz! How nice of you to drop in to see us!" The rest of the class who had by now all answered the register laughed. Then in a less sarcastic, more serious tone, the teacher said, "Your ten minutes late Fartz! Detention!"

Suffice to say it wasn't turning out to be a good day for poor little Eric, and the rest of the week didn't get any better either. The bullying didn't stop, and Eric was feeling down in the dumps. He now knew that the only way he was going to stop the bullying was if he stood up to them and put up a fight. Not literally, since he wasn't as big and physical as there were, but he would need to be cleverer and outsmart them, and not do something foolish like hand over his money to them. *(Never let fear misguide your common sense!)*

Much to Eric's relief, the weekend had finally arrived, so at least he would get a break from the bullying. His mum could tell her son was feeling down and upset. She thought it was probably just because she had confiscated his 'PlayStation'. "That's all it is," she said to herself. But she knew she couldn't go back on what she'd said already as that would undermine her authority and that could lead to all sorts of problems in the future. *(Never allow yourself to be intimidated by bullies and show weakness by letting them see that you are bothered and upset, otherwise they will do it even more!*

Bullies are cowards and only pick on those who are or appear to be weak and vulnerable, and with whom they think they can get away with it because they won't fight back.

Eric wasn't being bullied just because of his name or that he was short: it was because he lacked confidence and showed weakness and was therefore an easy target!

So, stand up for yourself, because by speaking up and being assertive, this will show you have confidence and that you are not frightened of them, and then they will be less likely to pick on you!

Also, by doing this: it will alert others around you to come to your aid and draw attention to the bullying — and that's the last thing they want!

But if you sense you are in danger — don't try to be a hero — flee to safety and seek help!)

CHAPTER THREE

CHRISTMAS MAGIC

It was now early December and people had already started to put up their Christmas decorations. Saturday morning, Ingrid had picked up a flyer whilst out doing some shopping, promoting a 'Christmas Fair' over the weekend at the local community centre. So, she thought to help cheer Eric up she would take him along to help pick out a new Christmas tree and some decorations as they'd left all their old ones in their house in Sheffield. They always bought a real tree and not one of those plastic imitation ones. It was a tradition in the Fartz family to always have a real one. It reminded her of the wonderful and happy

"This is my son, Eric."

"*Oh!* I've heard a lot about you Eric," said Carol. Eric just smiled.

Both women by now had got several bags of shopping in their hands and hanging off their wrists.

"Thank *God* for the plastic!" said Carol referring to her well-used credit card. They both laughed and got into a conversation. Eric started to get a little impatient and bored, nudging his mum slightly with his elbow.

"Mum, can we go?" asked Eric. His mum carried on chatting, and Eric could see he wasn't going to be able to separate them apart for some time. "Mum ... *Mum* ... *Mum!*" he kept calling out, trying to get her attention.

"What is it love?" his mum finally answered smiling with embarrassment at her son's interruption.

"Is it okay if I carry on having a look around?"

"Yes, of course, it is darling. I'll catch up with you in a minute," she replied and carried on chatting.

"Yeah right, and England will win the world cup!" he thought. Knowing that when his mum starts chatting it's never a minute. More like sixty!

So, Eric carried on along the aisle of glitter

and southern accents, trying to squeeze past people, and eventually he got to the end. There, right at the end, he could see lots of people, mostly children gathered around a stall. He couldn't tell what they were selling because of all the people blocking his view. But he kept hearing, "Oohs" and "Ah's" and lots of applause with the occasional laughter. Whatever was going on, the audience was having a great time, and Eric wanted to be a part of it. So, he squeezed through the crowd on his hands and knees and suddenly popped his head up at the front of the stall (this was the advantage of being small!).

"Hello! Who's this just suddenly *appeared* before us?" said a strange-looking man with a twinkle in his eye. He had a large crooked nose, a goatee beard, and wore an outdated top hat and a fancy waistcoat decorated with stars and moons. "Pick a card young man, any card you like," said the strange man behind the even stranger stall counter as he offered little Eric the choice of a card from the pack.

As Eric glanced around wide-eyed, bewildered at first by the odd-looking objects he saw displayed on the counter: shiny silver cups and balls; red sponge balls; packs of playing cards; various books; large fancy-looking boxes piled up one on top of the other;

and a black stick with white tips, he quickly realised he was at a magic shop stall. His face lit up and he smiled from ear to ear! He'd always liked watching magicians on the telly but had never seen a magician performing in person before.

All excited, Eric removed a card from the pack. The magician then asked him to look at the card and remember it, without showing it to him. Eric did as he was instructed and saw it was the nine of hearts. The card was returned, and the pack was thoroughly shuffled. The magician then held his fingertips to his forehead in a mystical fashion and said, "Think of your card." And after a dramatic pause the magician declared, "Your card is a red one, correct!" There was another pause. "The suit is a heart I believe." Eric nodded in amazement. Then after an even longer pause, the magician raised his voice and announced, "The card you are thinking of is the nine of hearts!"

"Yes!" said Eric, totally mesmerized and wondering how on earth this strange and captivating man wearing a top hat and a mystical waistcoat could have read his mind. Eric was speechless, which was not unusual for the usually quiet little Eric. It filled him with a sense of wonderment! And the whole crowd immediately burst into spontaneous applause.

The magician took a bow and then started his sales pitch, explaining that this is a 'Trick Pack of Cards' called the 'Svengali Pack', and with this amazing pack of cards, you can perform lots of amazing easy to do card trick miracles.

He then went on to demonstrate more amazing feats of magic you can perform with the special pack, causing Eric's chosen card to continually rise to the top after being placed into the middle. But it was the finale that really blew everybody's mind, when every single card turned into the nine of hearts! The crowd erupted into even louder applause this time shaking their heads in disbelief. To Eric, this was, real magic!

"I'll buy one!" called out one of the onlookers. Then somebody else said, "Yes, I'll buy one also, please," followed by somebody else wishing to buy one and another and another. In fact, everyone there bought a 'Svengali Pack', except for Eric, who couldn't afford one. He only had two pounds odd in his pocket, which is what he had left in his piggy bank after giving most of his savings to those two bullies. If only he hadn't of done that, he thought, then he could have bought a 'Svengali Pack' himself. He wanted one so badly. Maybe he could persuade his mum to buy him one, he then thought? Even if it meant not having the sweets that his mum promised him: because although he loved sweets just as much as any other kid would, Eric thought that he would much rather perform the amazing, card tricks he had just witnessed. It was no competition!

The crowd started to disperse, but not Eric, he wanted to see more. A spark went off in his brain and Eric was hooked. "Show me more, show me more!" said the thrilled and excitable boy.

The magician then showed Eric and other people who had just arrived even more mind-blowing magic tricks he sold at his shop. One such trick was a classic of magic called 'The Ball Vase', much to the delight of the audience, where with the wave of the magicians wand and some magic words, a little ball appeared and disappeared to and from an odd shaped little plastic cup. Several of the adults among the crowd remembered this trick from when they were children, having received it in a box set of magic tricks. After demonstrating that trick, he declared, "Here's a little miracle that anyone can do!" The magician then took a small red coloured silk handkerchief out of his waistcoat pocket and waved it in the air saying, "Watch the hankie!"

The magician proceeded to poke the hankie slowly, bit by bit, into the top of his fist, using each fingertip in turn, finally pushing it completely inside with his thumb. He made a magic gesture and then to everyone's surprise, when he opened his hand the hankie had disappeared! The audience once again applauded.

"What's that *stuck* on your thumb?" suddenly called out an unruly older child at the front, pointing at the magicians slightly swollen looking thumb. The magician quickly and slightly suspiciously, dived his hand into his trouser pocket, ignoring the remark and swiftly carried on with the next demonstration.

Next, to everyone's amazement, including the unruly boy, he turned a large die into lots of tiny dice! This one was called the 'Dice Smash', Eric noted. But still out of his price range.

The magician then demonstrated an astonishing magic trick called 'The Dynamic Coins' where a pile of coins appeared, transposed, penetrated and finally disappeared! Nobody had a clue how that trick was done. It completely baffled everyone! Eric really wanted to buy this trick too, in fact, he wanted to buy all the tricks, but alas he couldn't afford any of them. He would have to put them on his Christmas list he thought.

"What's that?" Eric asked the magician

curiously, pointing towards a gruesome looking miniature guillotine displayed on his stand.

"Ah, that is what is known as a Finger Chopper," replied the magician, chuckling to himself.

"A Finger Chopper!" exclaimed Eric, looking a little frightened.

The magician laughed. "Don't worry, it doesn't really chop your finger off," then explained the magician. "Watch, I'll show you." He raised the miniature guillotine's blade and then asked for a volunteer to place their finger through the hole. No one wanted to volunteer at first. "… Don't be frightened!" said the magician. And then a brave man cautiously extended his right forefinger and inserted it into the strange contraption.

Some people around the stand closed their eyes, but not Eric, as he wanted to watch. "On the count of three!" announced the magician. The volunteer quickly withdrew his finger and then to the sound of nervous laughter reluctantly reinserted it. You could feel the tension building! Everybody there joined in the counting, and upon the count of 'three' the magician sharply pushed the blade down. People screamed in horror as the blade appeared to go right through the volunteer's finger! The volunteer quickly removed his finger and examined it. And to much applause and relief, showed that no harm had come to it, not even a scratch. While the magician dramatically announced, "Lo and behold – the blade has passed through his finger without any harm!" Eric really liked that trick.

The magician then picked up a red velvet cloth bag with a wooden handle attached and turned it inside out showing there was nothing inside. "Prepare to be amazed!" he said in his mystical, slightly gravelly voice. He then gave Eric the magic wand and told him to wave it over the bag and say the magic word, 'Abracadabra'. But as Eric went to take the wand, it collapsed in his hand as if he'd broken it. "Oh dear!" said the magician. "What have you done to my magic wand?" Everybody laughed including Eric, who thought it was hilarious. Then to everyone's delight, the magician reached into the bag and pulled out lots of different coloured silk handkerchiefs, one by one, followed by what seemed to be a never-ending beautiful multi coloured silk streamer. The audience loved it and applauded loudly again.

The magician then thanked Eric for being a good sport and helping him. Some of the children who came to his magic stall were less helpful though. Sometimes they were naughty and rude, interrupting his performance by calling out how they thought the trick was done. The magician could see that Eric, however, was a polite boy and very enthusiastic about magic. So, he recommended he should take up magic as a hobby and gave him some good advice about performing magic. And as he'd helped him during some of his tricks, he gave him a free pack of 'Svengali Cards'. "Thank you very much!" replied Eric, delighted.

As the magician handed over the pack of cards, he then leant down and quietly whispered something in Eric's ear so only Eric could hear. What was it that was said? Was it a magic secret? Maybe the magician recognised in this boy something in himself when he was a child – something rare, that's inside all the best magicians perhaps? "*Don't* forget what I told you, will you, young man!" then said the wise old wizard as he left Eric to serve a customer down by the far end of the counter.

Eric was so glad he'd decided to come to the Christmas Fair after all. Any fears he had disappeared like magic on this day!

For the whole time he was there, which must have been at least half an hour, Eric had been completely transfixed and had forgotten all about his mum who was by now searching for him. Being small it was hard to spot him amongst the crowds. Then as she came past the magic stall again for the second time, she spotted her son through a slight gap in the crowd.

"Excuse me please!" she kept repeating as she squeezed past people, struggling with even more bags of shopping, on her way to the front of the stand. *"Eric!* I've been looking for you!" she said to him in somewhat of a fluster. "I was worried because I didn't know where you were!"

Still excited, Eric replied, "I've been here all the time watching lots of amazing magic tricks Mum. And *I* want to be a magician!" He held up the pack of cards the magician had given him and said, "Look, Mum, the magician gave me a free pack of magic cards for helping him!"

"Well done!" she told him. Well, when she saw how much fun he'd had and how happy he was, she decided to leave it at that. Besides her feet were now killing her after all that traipsing around Christmas shopping. "Let's go now and choose a nice Christmas tree!" she then said with a big smile. "I've bought you a bag of those sweets that you like love. I didn't forget!"

Eric thanked his mum and off they went together to buy a Christmas tree, calling out goodbye to the kind magician as they left. Eric helped his mum carry the shopping bags; it was less busy now and easier to move along the aisle.

When they got back outside, his mum looked inside her purse to see what money she had left as the man selling the Christmas trees would only accept cash. When she counted the money, she had only just enough left to buy the smallest tree there, which was about 4 foot high. Most of the other trees had already sold, which you could tell by all the spaces now along the wall. So, his mum bought it, and off they went back home. Eric had the job of carrying the tree and his mum carried the bags.

On their way home, Eric couldn't stop talking about all the mesmerising magic tricks that he had seen.

"You should have seen what he did with the playing cards! It was amazing!" he said to his mum excitedly, clearly inspired and eager to learn the tricks using his very own 'Svengali Pack'. "I can't wait to get home and practise!"

"I bet I can guess what you want for Christmas this year," said his mum smiling. Eric smiled back and nodded. His mum thought taking up magic as a hobby was a great idea for her son, as it would help him gain the confidence he lacked and be good for his social skills by getting out and meeting people. Therefore, she was all for it.

As they headed back across the playing fields, battling against the wind, carrying all the shopping, Eric could see two large boys in the distance kicking a football around. His immediate reaction was to instinctively cover his face with the Christmas tree, so they wouldn't see him. But then he bravely lowered the tree from his face, remembering what the magician had told him and walked the rest of the way home, believing he was a superhero!

CHAPTER FOUR

A NEW-FOUND PASSION

For the rest of the day, Eric spent most of the time in his bedroom with his door closed, learning the secret to the 'Svengali Pack' and how to perform the amazing card tricks, taught in the instructions, while his mum made a start with putting up the new Christmas decorations. Eric helped every now and then, between learning his magic tricks, and enjoyed decorating the tree with baubles and fairy lights and putting the star he had chosen on top of it – which he could only just about reach. His mum put some Christmassy music on and started singing along in her native tongue:

"Stille Nacht, heilige Nacht,
Alles schläft, einsam wacht
Nur das traute hockheilige Paar.
Holder Knabe im lockigen Haar,
Schlaf in himmlisher Ruh!
Schlaf in himmlisher Ruh! …"

Eric remembered fondly, the most enchanting story his mum used to tell, which her mother in Germany used to tell to her as a young child, about the fairies that lived in the Christmas tree and how it was the warmth from their bodies when they flapped their tiny wings that would generate enough heat and electricity to light up the tree! And would then explain, "That's why they are called 'Fairy Lights'!" As he reminisced, a big gleaming smile lit up his face! Both were very happy for a change.

"*Eric!* Britain's Got Talent is starting!" called out his mum as she hung another bauble on the tree. Eric normally never liked to miss it, but even his favourite TV show would not stop the protégé magician from learning his newfound passion. He practised and practised, over and over again, determined to get it right, sometimes getting frustrated as cards would fall to the floor and would then have to pick them up and start again. Quoted in the instructions, and what he'd often heard his mum say, Eric had read: 'Practice makes perfect!' and 'If at first, you don't succeed try, try again!' *(Two old proverbs worth remembering! You should always practise and rehearse your magic tricks before you perform them, so that you don't make mistakes and ruin the trick by revealing the secret!)*

It was getting late in the evening by now and even though he desperately wanted to show his mum the card tricks he had learned, it had been an exhausting day and he was feeling rather tired. So, he called out "Goodnight" to his mum and fell straight to sleep still holding the pack of cards in his hand.

Sunday morning Eric woke up around 8 am to find just about all the cards were now scattered in a mess on the floor by his bedside – some cards were face up and some face down: having relaxed his fingers as he drifted off to sleep the cards cascaded from his grip, flowing off his bed like a waterfall. No nightmare this time, but instead, he had a very pleasant dream of him standing on stage in front of lots of people performing an amazing magic act with everybody cheering and applauding him. He had just won 'Britain's Got Talent'! And that's when he woke up. He jumped out of bed with a big happy smile and reassembled his pack of cherished magic cards, carefully putting them back in their case.

Now armed with his special deck of cards in his hand again, he went in search of his first ever volunteer, his mum, who didn't take long to find in their tiny flat.

"Guten Morgen! I'm in *here!"* called out his mum in her native German tongue. Eric found his mum sat at the dining table finishing her breakfast cereal.

"Mum! Pick a card, any card you like –" said the very eager protégé magician as he offered her the choice of a card.

"Have your breakfast first love," she said chuckling and admiring her son's enthusiasm at such an early time on Sunday morning. To Eric that was like someone firing a starting pistol at the start of a race. And Eric had already left the blocks! He gulped his cereal down as fast as he could, some missing his mouth completely. He even declined the offer of toast with peanut butter, which he normally loves. "Wow! You made that disappear quickly!" laughed his mum, thinking she was being very witty with her reference to magic.

With food still in his mouth, Eric offered his mum the choice of a playing card again.

"Pick a card, any card you like ..." Eric repeated. He had remembered virtually all the patter the magician had said during his demonstration yesterday and went on to perform a couple of the tricks he had learnt from the instructions. There are so many tricks one can perform with 'The Svengali Pack' and Eric performed the same trick he had seen the magician perform at the Christmas Fair called, 'The Ambitious Card', where the chosen card despite being placed in the middle of the pack, repeatedly rises to the top! His mum was well impressed!

Eric then performed another incredible trick where the chosen card is seemingly lost in the pack, and as the magician deals the cards, one card at a time, face down onto the table, the spectator is asked to call out "Stop" at any time they like. And when the card is turned over, it is revealed to be the chosen one! (Both these card tricks are classics of magic and performed with a regular pack of cards using skilful sleight of hand, but using the 'Svengali Pack' makes it easier to perform these amazing tricks.)

"Can I show you one more trick please Mum?" asked Eric still buzzing with excitement.

"Yes, alright darling," she replied pleased to see her son so enthusiastic.

"You see all the cards are differ—"

"What's that burning smell?" suddenly said his mum, interrupting him. "Oh 'eck! It's the toast!"

She quickly went and switched the grill pan off and threw the blackened toast in the waste bin. She had been so transfixed by her sons incredible magic tricks that she had forgotten all about the toast. "Panic over! Go ahead," she said. Then suddenly the smoke alarm went off, startling them both. "… Nevermind, carry on Son!" she then called out over the sound of the noisy alarm. So, undeterred, Eric performed his finale, miraculously causing all of the playing cards to turn into her chosen card, whilst his mum was at the same time standing on tiptoes and waving the tea-towel frantically around in the air trying to perform her own magic trick and make the smoke disappear!

Finally, the smoke dispersed, the beeping stopped, and his mum gave him a big round of applause, pleasantly surprised at how good he was. What an eventful morning it was turning out to be!

"How did you do that?" she said amazed and impressed that he had learnt these magic tricks so quickly!

"A good magician never reveals his secrets!" he replied, which is one of the rules of magic he had read in the instructions. *(Yes, that's right because if you reveal the secret, it will no longer be special, and it would spoil it for your spectators. Plus, you will get less credit as a magician!)*

"Actually, I don't want to know how you did it because then it would spoil it! Well done love!" said his mum still in amazement.

He did make a few minor mistakes whilst performing the tricks, but his mum pretended not to see those, and just gave him praise and encouragement. She thought he'd done brilliantly, especially as it was the first time that he'd ever performed magic.

"I have arranged to go and see my friends for afternoon tea at one of their houses. Why don't you come along and perform your magic for everyone!" said his Mum thinking what a good idea that would be.

"… Erm, yes, alright," said Eric in an enthusiastic, albeit slightly nervous way.

"Their children will be there also," his mum added thinking it would be good for her son also to mix with other children.

"I'm going to my room to practise Mum."

Eric started to head for his bedroom when his mum suddenly said, "Wait a moment Eric, I have something for you?" His mum reached into her large bag searching for something.

"What is it Mum?" enquired Eric inquisitively, wondering what it could be? His mum then handed him a book, but not just any book, it was a magic book for beginners. "A magic book!" shrieked Eric delighted, "Oh, thank you, Mum!" His mum had secretly gone back to the magic shop stall, leaving Eric waiting at the entrance, telling him a little white lie that she had forgotten to buy something. She had intended to wrap the book and give it to him as a Christmas present, but she could see how interested he was in magic and so decided to give it to him that morning.

Eric went off to his room and promptly closed the door behind him, while his mum got on with some household chores, singing merrily along to herself as she did. His appetite had been wetted and he wanted to learn more magic tricks, like the one's the magician he was so inspired by, performed the day before. He was so excited and immediately sat down on the edge of his unmade bed and started reading.

He had never had a magic book before. He turned one of the pages and came across the heading 'The French Drop', "Oh, that looks interesting!" he thought. It was a technique on how to make a coin disappear. It reminded him of when the magic shop owner would go to give a customer their change and, just for fun, would suddenly make it disappear! Of course, moments later he did give the change back. Eric thought this would be a fun trick to perform and began learning how to make a coin disappear! *(To learn the secret to this amazing trick, and, many more, go through the locked door to 'Eric's Magic Trick Secrets' at the end of the story. Oh, and don't forget to bring your imagination with you!)*

He must have read through the explanation at least half a dozen times just to make sure he understood it. Eric practised the coin vanish in front of the mirror to start with, as was advised in the book. He kept dropping the coin at first but would pick it up and kept practising. He even amazed himself when he looked at his reflection in the mirror. He was now the proud owner of his very first magic book and he was delighted! *(It is recommended to read 'Magic Books' as well as watching magic taught on video, because although it is good to watch other magicians teaching you on video to see how others perform the tricks, by reading books you will find that you will use your imagination more and will, therefore, be more creative and your presentation will be more original. After all, you don't want to be a carbon copy of another magician!)*

CHAPTER FIVE

A SURPRISING AFTRENOON TEA

"*ric!* It's *time* to go, love!" called out his mum.

"Mum, I've changed my mind – I don't want to go," he replied, sounding anxious as he approached her.

"Oh, don't worry – everyone will love your magic tricks – you'll be great!" she replied, trying her best to encourage him.

"But, what if I mess up the tricks?"

"You won't sweetheart – now come on, it will do you good."

So, after some gentle coaxing, Eric reluctantly picked up his magic cards and they both headed off to her friend Carol's house.

Carol was originally from Wales and moved there with her family several years ago.

It was cold outside, but the wind had dropped, and the sun was out. Much nicer than it was the day before. The house they were visiting wasn't very far away. Ingrid hadn't been there before and was really looking forward to having a nice chat with her friends from work.

"I think this is the one," she said. It was a nice looking three-bedroom house on one of those modern housing estates. All the lawns were perfectly manicured with gleaming and sparklingly clean family cars on the driveways.

They could hear a lot of noise coming from inside, so they thought this is probably the correct address.

"Eric do you want to ring the bell?" asked his mum. Eric reached up high and rang the bell. Suddenly they heard a loud barking and clawing sound on the other side of the door. As the front door opened, a hairy leg suddenly popped into view.

"Hello!" said a Welsh voice from behind the door. It was Carol, desperately struggling to hold back the dog and stop it keep jumping up. It was the families pit bull terrier. "Do come in," she said, while still trying to remain calm and speak posh. Both Eric and his mum looked

a bit hesitant and frightened.

"*Hiya* Carol!" said Ingrid with a slight quiver in her voice as the dog continued to growl and bark. "How are you?"

"Fine, thanks!" replied Carol, forcing a smile.

"What's your dog's name?" asked Ingrid trying to look unaffected.

"This is Killa – spelt with an 'a'," Carol quickly answered, still trying to keep control of it.

"Oh!" just muttered Ingrid, looking even more frightened, while Eric looked on equally so.

"Oh, don't worry about Killa. We've just had him castrated and he's a bit grumpy today," said Carol as she bent down and gave the dog a quick cuddle and kissed him on the head. "You are a grumpy dog today aren't you Killa. *Yes,* you *are! Yes,* you *are!*" repeated Carol as if she was talking to a small child and not a dog. Carol pulled the barking dog away by its collar, struggling to control it, so the visitors could come in. "I'll put him in the front room for now until he settles down."

Ingrid was thinking, "I hope she keeps him there!" As they entered the hallway, they could also hear loud gunfire and explosion noises coming from upstairs. It was very noisy and chaotic.

"I like all your Christmas decorations!" Ingrid commented to Carol. "Aren't they lovely Eric ... *Eric,* aren't they lovely?" Ingrid repeated, giving him a slight nudge. Eric was miles away.

"Yeah," Eric then just replied.

"Thank you, dears," replied Carol, pleased to keep hearing it each time her guests arrived. Carol certainly went to town when it came to Christmas decorations, not wanting to be out down by the neighbours. There were decorations everywhere – even the decorations had decorations! And their Christmas tree was more than twice the size of the Fartz's tree.

"We're all in the conservatory – come on through," said Carol in a bit of a fluster, her hair, less tidy than before she went to answer the door. Eric followed his mum into the conservatory eager to show more people the magic tricks he'd learnt.

In the room, there were Ingrid's other newly found friends Julie and Fiona with their children. "Hello!" everyone said in unison. It was a bit of a tight squeeze in there, but they managed. The men were all still down the pub.

Each of the mums introduced their children, followed lastly by Carol. "And these are my two – Anna and Megan, and my oldest boy, Gary, is upstairs in his bedroom trying to save

the world from being taken over by zombies."
Laughter ensued.

Laid out neatly on the coffee table, were a
variety of freshly cut sandwiches and a choice
of 'Victoria Sponge Cake' or 'Chocolate Cake',
which all the children kept eyeing up. All the
adults immediately started chatting to one
another and the children, who already knew
each another, started playing a board game in a
corner of the room. Except Eric, who was sat
on the floor staring against a wall, analysing
when would be the best time to perform his
magic show? He thought it was probably best
to perform after people had eaten. Also, he
didn't feel quite up to it yet.

His mum saw Eric was by himself and
looking slightly uneasy. The nerves had started
to kick in. So she said, "Why don't you join in
with the other children Eric?"

"Why does my Mum *always* say embarrassing
stuff like that?" he thought, much to his
annoyance. The other children were two or
three years younger than him and he didn't
think that would look cool. "I'm fine Mum,"
he replied rather abruptly. Besides, Eric was
still thinking about his performance and what
trick he should perform first.

"Isn't your boy shy, Ingrid?" Carol said to no
reply. Just a polite smile, not realising that she

had hit a nerve by making that comment to Ingrid. "… Right, is everyone ready for a cup of tea and a slice of cake?" asked Carol struggling to get up from her seat. Carol was a rather large lady who clearly liked her splodgy cream cakes. "I'll go and put the kettle on."

Before going into her plush new fitted kitchen to make a pot of tea she called up to her son Gary from the hallway. *"Gary* darling! Would you like to come and join us for tea and cake? I bought your favourite chocolate cake you like …" She had to ask him again because the noise from the video game was so loud, and the dog started barking again.

"No! I told you, I *don't* want to. Are you *deaf?"* Gary eventually replied very rudely. *"I'm* playing video games, leave me *be!"*

"Would you like me to save you some cake?" his mum called up.

"YES! NOW STOP DISTURBING ME! OH! NOW YOU'VE MADE ME GET EATEN!" The rude boy screamed down to his mum even louder in his high-pitched Welsh accent. Everyone could hear him. His mum thought it best to leave him to it so he wouldn't have one of his temper tantrums. Her son had anger issues.

Meanwhile, in the conservatory, apart from a few raised eyebrows, the adults continued chatting – mostly about the latest gossip at work. And the children continued playing their game, laughing and giggling every so often. Everyone was having a jolly time. Well, everyone except Eric, who was now staring at a framed photograph on the wall he had just spotted of someone he immediately recognized dressed in his school uniform. It was one of the bullies – 'Hamburger'! Whose real name was Gary!

"OH NO! GET ME OUT OF HERE!" was the immediate reaction he screamed in his head as that overwhelming feeling of dread once again started to envelop him. The poor little fellow started to panic for a moment not knowing *what* to do. But, for a change, he didn't show any obvious signs of fear. Eric kept calm by repeating to himself what the magician at the magic stall had confided in him. Before the weekend if he'd been faced with this situation he would probably have run for the door! So, his confidence must have improved.

Anyway, he had a job to do, put on a magic show and amaze everyone! At that point, Carol came in carrying a tray with a large pot of tea, cups and saucers and a pile of plates.

"Here we are," she said as she put the tray onto the table. "Now, who's ready to eat?"

All the younger kids screamed "Yeah!"

"Please help yourselves to sandwiches and cake ... I better just cut off a slice of Gary's favourite chocolate cake for him," she added. Well, Carol must have cut off a third of the cake for him. Everyone looked at each other in surprise.

Carol carried on being her usual chirpy self as if the episode with her son just then hadn't happened – it was as if she was used to it. Eric wasn't the only person to be bullied by Gary – Gary's mum was too! Carol was far too soft with her son, always pampering him, and often letting him get away with how he treated her. Her husband wasn't much better either. He often worked away from home as a long-distance lorry driver or was out with his mates drinking, leaving poor Carol to mostly deal with his poor behaviour.

"I like your pink furry slippers," said Ingrid to Carol, noticing them on the floor.

Carol laughed, saying, "Oh, they're not *mine* – they're *Gary's!* He got a thing for pink and just loves the soft feel of them for some reason?" Upon hearing this, Eric's ears pricked and his eyebrows raised involuntarily. "He's a big softy really!"

"He's *big* alright, but a softy?" thought Eric, overhearing the conversation.

"Is Gary not coming down to join us?" said

Julie.

"No, he's happy where he is, bless him," Carol replied smiling with a tinge of embarrassment, quickly changing the subject. *'More* tea anyone?"

Eric gave a big sigh of relief that 'Hamburger' wasn't going to be joining them.

By now all the guests were tucking into their plate of sandwiches and cakes and thoroughly enjoying them.

"Did you make these yourself? Their lovely!" said Ingrid. Everyone else had their mouth's full and just nodded in agreement.

"Yes!" replied Carol, smiling broadly. She was telling porkies – she bought them from ASDA up the road! Carol always liked to make a good impression even if it meant telling a little white lie occasionally.

Carol could see that Eric didn't want to join in with the other younger children and was bored. So, she said to him, "Eric, after you've finished eating, why don't you go upstairs and play video games with Gary?" Eric suddenly froze, not saying a word.

Ingrid could see that her son was keen to start his magic show. So, spoke for him in a proud 'Dance Mom', or in her case, 'Magic Mom' kind of voice, and said, "Eric would like to put on a magic show for you all!" On hearing that, everyone, especially the younger children got excited and moved to get a better position. The draft caused from the sudden rush of bodies nearly blowing over some of the carefully placed Christmas cards situated around the room. They all sat crowded together on the fake suede, tan coloured, furniture, with some of the kids spilling off onto the floor by the feet of their mums ready to watch the performance.

Eric was naturally nervous to start with, and as he pulled the pack of cards out of his pocket, he accidentally dropped it on the floor, and a few cards slid out of the box. Some of the younger children giggled followed by the sound of "Shh!" from their mums. But Eric smiled and carried on as he removed the rest of the cards from the box.

"I'd like to show you some card tricks," quietly announced Eric. He showed the cards to be all different and then proceeded to have one selected. Eric then performed a couple of the mind-boggling card tricks he had learnt with the 'Svengali Pack', which he had shown his mum earlier. Only this time, he didn't make any mistakes. Everyone watching cheered and applauded as he finished performing each trick, which kept waking up the dog, who would then bark loud each time. The mums all looked at each with raised eyebrows, clearly impressed and surprised at how a normally quiet boy was now confidently standing up in front of them and performing these amazing, magic tricks!

Eric's confidence grew and grew, and by now he was enjoying himself so much that he completely forgotten about 'Hamburger' being upstairs. Feeling a lot more confident, he decided to perform another magic trick. This time one he had learnt from his new magic book and picked up a silver teaspoon from one of the saucers.

"Carol did you know that your spoons are made of rubber!" Suiting the actions to the words, he pressed the bowl of the spoon against the table and appeared to bend it almost in half.

"Oh dear, what have you done to my nice spoon!" said Carol genuinely worried for a moment. Everybody else began to laugh.

"Don't worry! I am a magician!" said Eric as he covered the damaged spoon with his hands and wiggled his fingers. "... Abracadabra!" Eric lifted his hands away and to everyone's amazement the spoon was completely restored!" Everyone burst into loud, spontaneous applause, drowning out the sounds of the dog barking and the gunfire coming from upstairs. (*Learn the secret to 'The*

Rubber Spoon' trick at the rear of the book)

Eric thanked everyone and took a bow, but the children all chanted, "Do one more trick! Do one more trick!" The novice magician wanted to perform the 'Vanishing Coin Trick' but didn't feel he was quite ready to perform that one just yet. He thought it still needed a bit more practice. He could only remember one other trick he had learnt, which was a mind reading trick. So, he decided to perform that trick instead.

He gave Julie a small square of paper with a circle drawn on it, and turning his head away said, "Would you please secretly write down the name of a famous person, dead or alive, in the circle I have drawn, but don't tell me or let me see what you are writing."

So, after giving it some thought, she wrote down the name of her favourite singer, 'Elvis Presley', being careful not to let Eric she what she had put. Eric then requested her to, "Fold the paper into quarters so I can't see what you've written ..." All said in a very serious and dramatic manner just like how he remembered seeing 'Mind Readers' on the telly.

Still with his head turned away he took the folded paper back from Julie and tore it up into tiny pieces. "... We won't need this anymore," he said and threw the bits of paper away.

Holding one of his hands to his forehead, he looked at Julie mysterious like, and said, "Now look into my eyes and concentrate on the name of the famous person you chose."

Except for the distant noise coming from 'Hamburger's' bedroom, the room went completely silent – even the dog stopped barking for a moment.

"Try to visualize this person ..." he added as Julie concentrated, trying to keep a straight face, unsure whether she should take it seriously or not. Then after a dramatic pause, he announced "The name of the person you are thinking of is ..." Another dramatic pause. "Elvis!" The audience was stunned, especially Julie, and as Eric took his final bow, everyone burst into loud spontaneous applause once more! How could Eric have known that? *(Find out how to read people's minds at the rear of the book! The trick is called 'The Centre Tear')*

And, as the magic show came to an end, so did this wonderous afternoon tea party. As people were leaving, they were all praising Eric on his performance. The children were still pestering him to perform more! Eric's mum gave him a big hug and said she was very proud of him. Ingrid thanked Carol for inviting them and both said goodbye to everyone. They then left as they entered to the loud sounds of the dog barking, gunfire and explosions.

Eric's confidence had stated to grow, and as they walked back home together, he felt as tall as the enormous Christmas tree that greeted them at the Christmas Fair!

"Everyone was surprised at how good you were Eric!" said his proud mum.

"It had been an afternoon full of surprises alright!" thought Eric.

CHAPTER SIX

ERIC FORMS A NEW FRIENDSHIP

They both arrived back home from Carol's house. Eric's mum put the dinner on and Eric, a little tired but still elated by the great response he got from performing his magic show, went straight to his room to learn more magic tricks.

He still couldn't believe that his mums best friends' son was one of the bullies! Eric tried not to focus on it but every now and then kept getting flashing images in his head of the grossly overweight 'Hamburger' wearing pink furry slippers. He would shake his head each time to try and get the image out of his head, and every now and then burst into spontaneous laughter.

"What were you laughing about?" asked his mum inquisitively.

"Oh nothing!" replied Eric, smiling.

During dinner they both talked about what a wonderful day it had been and Eric's mum said, "You can have your PlayStation back and play video games tonight if you like Son." But Eric wasn't interested in that anymore and only wanted to learn and practise more tricks.

Eric quickly finished his desert, which he hadn't lost interest in, and jumped up from his seat and went straight back to his magic den. His mum was pleased that he had now found another pastime rather than playing video games all the time.

The next morning Eric went off to school and his mum went off to work. On the way there, Eric bumped into his classmate Jack Robinson. By now the two of them had got to know each other better by spending a few detentions together. Jack had never really noticed Eric before that.

As they made their way to school, Eric would jump every now and again to avoid stepping on the cracks in the pavement. The superstitious behaviour he probably picked up from his mum. Superstitions, fears and anxieties, and self-doubts are often passed on from generation to generation. "It's unlucky to walk under a ladder!" and "Thirteen is an unlucky number!" he would sometimes hear his mum say. *(Don't allow other people's irrational and unfounded fears and anxieties to be passed onto you. As fear can prevent you from achieving your goals and ambitions in life! If you believed all the superstitions and fears you heard, you wouldn't do anything – you'd be too frightened to even leave the house!*

If you think about it rationally and logically: walking under a ladder, for instance, is not unlucky in the sense that something bad might happen to you in the future, as it is largely perceived to mean – it's because the ladder might accidentally fall on top your head! (Ouch!)

As with most superstitions: it is told with the intention of protecting you and merely to prevent you from the risk of danger and harm by striking fear into you, which is sensible and sage advice and nothing more! But also, fearmongering, which plays on people's fears and anxieties, has been used throughout history, and still to this day, as a means to control people!)

Eric and Jack got on very well and had a similar sense of humour. Jack, however, by contrast, was a confident and very popular boy, deemed as one of the cool kids and part of the 'In crowd', who loved sports and was tall and well built, unlike Eric. Jack was in all the school sports teams and especially liked rugby.

Eric noticed that Jack had a couple of elastic

bands wrapped tightly around his shoe to prevent the sole from flapping open.

"Jack, can I borrow those elastic bands you have around your shoe for a minute? I'll show you a magic trick," said Eric.

Jack laughed, slightly out of embarrassment, "Sure!" and removed the two elastic bands and gave them to Eric. "Make sure you don't snap 'em!"

"I won't, I promise!" replied Eric. He then performed an astonishing magic trick, causing the two elastic bands to link and unlink in a most magical and mystifying way.

"How did you do that?" Jack said amazed. "That was *sick!*"

"It's a secret!" replied Eric smiling.

"Can you repair my shoe by magic?" joked Jack.

Jack thought Eric was cool and was pleased to call him his friend. The magic trick he had shown him was a simple trick with just two elastic bands called 'The Linking Rubber Bands'. *(Find out the secret to this incredible trick at the rear of the book).*

On the way to school, they passed by the community centre where Eric had been to the Christmas Fair over the weekend.

"I went to a Christmas Fair there on Saturday and there was a sick magic shop stall there," said Eric. Eric had often heard Jack use the word 'sick' to mean cool. So, decided he would adopt that word too. "Did you go Jack?"

"No," replied Jack, shaking his head and sounding disappointed. "I *wish,* but I had to do some chores."

The community centre looked very different now though. The shabby entrance door was locked. No garish decorations hanging up. No Christmas trees lining the walls outside. No carol singers singing along to joyful festive music. And the happy smiling faces were replaced by miserable looking ones of people waiting outside at the bus stop. Still buzzing with new-found confidence, Eric went over and showed them a quick magic trick, and as if by magic, smiles appeared on their faces, and for a moment they seemed to have forgotten all about their worries and woes.

Eric couldn't wait to show more people his magic. He liked the response you get from performing magic and found it very rewarding and empowering. And during the school mid-morning break that day, while he was in the playground, he plucked up the courage to perform his amazing magic to other children in his year. Before he knew it, pupils prized their eyes away from their mobile phone screens and looked on in wonder as he performed his astonishing magic tricks, as if transfixed and under his spell, completely forgetting about their mobile phones!

He got quite a crowd around him in the playground watching and applauding him, even some of the children who had called him names in the past joined in the applause. He got, the occasional, "I know how you did that trick!" type of remarks. Mainly from kids who were only pretending they knew to sound clever in front of their friends.

It caused quite a commotion, and one of the teachers on break duty came over to see what was happening and to make sure that there wasn't a fight going on. At the unusual sight of all the pupils refraining from staring at their mobile phone screens for a change, the teacher thought, "Now that is what I call magic!"

The bell was heard, which meant that the mid-morning break was now over, and Eric, Jack and a few other classmates, who now also wanted to be Eric's friend, went off to their lessons together.

"Oh, I've just remembered! I've got to get a textbook from my locker. See you later!" said Eric as he rushed off.

"Yeah, see you later!" replied his new friend Jack. Eric hadn't seen the two bullies at school and thought that they were probably playing truant again. But when Eric closed his locker door, to his surprise, there they were standing behind it as if they had just appeared by magic. They gave him the fright of his life.

"Watcha Fartz! Ahh, did we make you jump?" said the bully David, as cocky as usual.

"Ahh, did we make you jump?" chimed in 'Hamburger', repeating what David had just said while chomping on a mouthful of his egg mayonnaise sandwich, and burping in Eric's face. His bad breath made Eric wince.

"Will you *stop* keep repeating everything I say!" David quickly said to 'Hamburger', finding it annoying. He then continued addressing Eric. "If you don't hand over your dinner money *now*, you'll get much worse happen to ya than us making you jump!" said David as he pulled a menacing face and punched the locker right next to Eric's head, creating a loud bang and making Eric jump again.

"Okay, okay, I'll get it for you," said a now frightened and distressed Eric. To David, Eric was just a 'Cash Machine' that he could draw money out of whenever he wanted – only, instead of using a bank card, he put his fist in to get cash out!

David backed off a little bit as Eric reached it his pocket and pulled out all the money he had, which he was supposed to pay for his dinner with. As he was removing the coins from his trouser pocket, his inner voice kept telling him, "DO THE 'FRENCH DROP'! DO THE 'FRENCH DROP'! DON'T LET THEM HAVE IT!" It was like the magician at the Christmas Fair was speaking to him.

Eric had practised the 'Coin Vanish Move' a lot more by now, and bravely as he went to hand over his dinner money to David, he did the 'French Drop', and upon opening his hand all the coins had vanished!

The two bullies both stepped back in stunned silence completely surprised at what just happened and were lost for words for a change! 'Hamburger' even sort of smiled, like he forgot for a moment to be 'The Bully' and enjoyed that moment of amazement. The smile soon dropped though as he caught David's glance towards him.

Then David, clearly irritated and annoyed at the thought of being fooled by his victim, said in a frustrated and condescending tone, "It's *obvious,* it's in your other hand!"

The two bullies were now staring intently at Eric's other hand thinking that they had caught Eric out, but then Eric slowly opened his hand to show that there were no coins there either. David was completely dumbfounded and looked crestfallen.

'Hamburger' started to smile again in wonder, and then laughed at David, saying in his irritating voice, "He's just *mugged* you off!"

"*Shut it!*" snapped back David angrily, giving 'Hamburger' a 'dead arm' with his tightly clenched fist.

"OUCH!" screamed 'Hamburger', feeling the pain and no longer laughing as he rubbed his sore arm.

While the two bullies were still bickering and stunned by what just happened, Eric sharply turned on his heels and deftly slipped away and headed off to his geography class, which Eric normally hated but, on this occasion had never got there as quick!

Eric had fooled his enemy and was very pleased with himself as he sat down and began to take notes on irrigation systems in West Africa. He was especially pleased as he had pulled off the 'French Drop' technique so well, seemingly vanishing the coins. But he also realised that he'd only just escaped by the skin of his teeth and knew this probably wasn't the end of it.

After his geography lesson, the school lunch bell rang and off he went to the dining hall. And for a change would be able a school dinner that day. Eric was sat around a table with Jack and a couple of his rugby teammates. Jack asked him to perform some magic. So, Eric performed a few tricks for them including the 'Bending Spoon' trick with their spoons, causing much hilarity and amazement.

And then, Eric picked up a napkin, holding it by the top two corners and draped it over a bowl of bread rolls in front of him, "What's he going to do now?" thought the bedazzled onlookers. Suddenly one of the bread rolls rose up from out of the bowl under the handkerchief, with its shape clearly seen. Eric struggled to keep control of it at one point, as the roll seemed to want to fly away dragging Eric up from his seat. Everyone looked on in amazement and by now even pupils on other tables started to take notice.

Eric noticed a pretty girl with long black hair on the adjacent table constantly smiling at him and enjoying his antics with the bread roll. It was a girl in his class called Emily, but who he had never spoken to before because he felt too shy. Eric smiled back at her still struggling with the bread roll as it darted here and there above the table. The roll then suddenly popped halfway into view momentarily above the top of the napkin causing a sudden gasp from around the dining room. The roll then went back under the napkin and floated back down and nestled back in the bowl. Eric whipped the napkin away to the joyful sound of cheers and applause. One of the pupils at the table immediately grabbed the roll out of the bowl, cautiously examined it, and took a big bite out of it causing everyone at the table to laugh out loud. *(Learn the secret to 'The Floating Bread Roll' at the rear of the book.)*

"*Quieten* down!" shouted out one of the dinner monitors. Eric then thanked his audience of fellow diners, thinking he'd now get to eat his meal, but now pupils from the adjacent tables wanted to watch him too.

"Show us another trick!" someone at the table called out, ignoring the dinner monitor's pleas to be quiet.

"Okay, okay, sure," Eric replied, taking a quick bite out of a boiled potato before carrying on. Eric asked to borrow a coin and covered it on the table with an upturned clear plastic tumbler. He explained, "To shroud the secret in mystery I shall cover the tumbler with this napkin." Once he'd done that, he then announced. "I shall cause the coin to penetrate through the solid table!" He said the magic word 'Abracadabra' and lifted the tumbler, but the coin was still there. "Oh!" he said and covered the coin once again. His friends laughed thinking the trick had gone wrong, but after a bit of friendly banter, Eric suddenly smashed the palm of his hand against the top of the tumbler, squashing the napkin flat on the table. The tumbler was gone! Sounds of amazement were heard, followed by cheering and applauding. Eric was getting used to hearing that wonderful sound and liked it a lot.

"Oh … my … *gosh!*" someone screamed.

Eric then coolly reached under the table and brought the tumbler up into view. The tumbler, it would seem had passed right through the solid table instead! *(Learn how to cause a glass to pass through a solid table at the rear of the book. The trick is called 'The Glass Through the Table'.)*

The school bell did its job indicating it was the end of the lunch break and all the children went off to their respective classes. Those that watched Eric perform were still talking about how amazed they were. "He's like that magician on the T.V!" someone said.

As Eric and his new friends were leaving, Eric heard a voice from behind him say, "I really liked your magic tricks!" It was Emily, the pretty girl who had been admiring his magic. Eric turned around.

"Thank you," said Eric. He then realised who it was and went a bit quiet and shy.

"My name is Emily. Emily Ryan. What's your

name?" Eric already knew her name and just stared into her beautiful brown eyes, speechless for a moment. The girl laughed, "Have you forgotten your name?"

"… Eric. I'm Eric," he said, bottling up enough courage to just about be able to get his name out.

"Are you coming?" called out Jack who was now way ahead of him.

"Yeah, hold on!" replied Eric.

"Bye then, nice to meet you," said Emily smiling.

"Tarra! See ya in class," said Eric slightly more confidently. Emily nodded and Eric quickly turned and run after his friend, smiling broadly as he did.

Jack teased Eric giving him a nudge, "I think she fancies you mate,"

"No, she doesn't, get out of here," said Eric still beaming.

"You fancy her too, don't cha," said Jack grinning, sure that he was right.

"Do I 'eckers like. Shurup up Jack!" replied Eric in his northern dialect, still smiling away, but slightly red-faced and embarrassed as both the boys headed off to the classroom.

The school day had come to an end, and Eric met up with his friend Jack who he had invited to come back to his flat after school. As Eric and Jack were leaving, Eric noticed that the two bullies, David and 'Hamburger' were standing by the gates, probably waiting for him – 'Hamburger' was forcing a whole chocolate bar into his mouth at the time.

The two cowardly bullies did not dare try anything on while Eric was with Jack because they knew Jack was a popular boy at school, and they wouldn't stand a chance against him in a fight. So, both the two bullies carried on talking to each other pretending not to notice Eric and Jack as they walked past them. Both, unconsciously bursting the pus from their spots; both, wondering how come Jack is now a friend with that loser Eric?

"What's he doing with that *Northern* Muppet?" said 'Hamburger', trying to act hard in front of David.

"The expression is Northern Monkey, *not* Muppet! You *Muppet!*" replied David, still peeved he hadn't managed to collect Eric's dinner money earlier that day.

"Oh!" just grunted 'Hamburger' in reply. He then started picking his nose and pulled out a great big slimy 'greeny' on the tip of his forefinger he'd been saving all day. "Hey, watch me make *this* disappear!" he then said as he promptly ate it.

Just then Emily walked by. *"Watcha*

gorgeous!" David called out to her, trying to act cool, but she just ignored him and walked straight by.

"… You've just been *pied!*" said 'Hamburger', laughing.

"*Shut it!*" snarled David, holding his fist up and threatening to punch him. David was then suddenly aware of a horrible smell. "… Oh! Have you just farted again Hamburger?" said David to his grinning friend. "... Oh, it stinks!" added David, holding his nose. 'Hamburger' just burst out laughing again, seeming to relish the smell of his own farts, and popped another chocolate bar in his gob.

It was Monday and his mum always cooked 'Bratkartoffeln' on a Monday. Both boys could smell the pleasant aroma as they walked up the shared garden path to the flat.

As they entered at the side kitchen door Eric called out, "Um, smells good!" He had got used to that smell and knew exactly what it was.

"Hiya love!" called out his mum. She then noticed the other boy as he entered the kitchen as well. "Oh hiya, who's this then, Eric?"

"This is my friend Jack. Is it alright if he stays for tea?" Eric asked, knowing that his mum always cooked more than enough food.

"Course it is! Nice to meet you, Jack," she said, giving him a warm and welcoming smile.

"Nice to meet you too Mrs Fartz," replied Jack in a confident and polite manner, assuming she was married. Ingrid didn't bother to correct him on her marital status, as was often the case, to avoid people asking too many questions. "I like your Christmas decorations!" then said Jack admiringly. "We haven't put ours up yet."

"Thank you, love. Oh, I love Christmas!" replied Eric's mum thinking what a nice polite lad he is.

She was very pleased that her son had found a friend in their new town of Ramsgate. "Have you shown Jack any of your magic tricks yet Eric?" she then asked. Eric nodded and smiled.

"Yes, his magic tricks are amazing!" said Jack, smiling enthusiastically. "I haven't got a clue how he does 'em!"

"Me neither!" she agreed.

"He won't tell me the secrets," said Jack.

"He won't tell me the secrets either. And I'm his *mum!*" she replied laughing.

"A good magician never reveals his secrets!" Eric reminded them.

His mum carried on with the cooking and Eric and his new friend Jack took a football outside for a kick about until teatime. She could hear them laughing together and having a great time. Jack had been ribbing Eric again about how he and Emily fancied each other.

It was now Jack's turn to show Eric his skills at 'Keepy Uppies'. Eric was equally impressed at Jack's skills with a ball as Jack was with his magic skills. He kept the ball in the air for ages and if it weren't for Eric's mum shouting "Dinners ready!" he would have probably kept the ball up for even longer!

"On my head!" Eric called out to Jack. Jack kicked the ball up in the air and as Eric went to head it, he missed the ball completely. Both boys burst into fits of laughter. They then went back inside the house to enjoy Eric's mum's skill at cooking.

"… This tastes delicious!" commented Jack, licking his lips. "Next time mate, you should come around to my house and try my mums 'Jerk Chicken'!" A new friendship had formed! *(Eric soon realised that the more confident and popular you were, the less chance there was of being bullied. And performing magic certainly helps with that and is a great way to be noticed and make friends! Bullies normally target individuals rather than those who have friends around them. Especially those who show a lack of confidence or are perceived as being weak or different! So, making friends will not only make life more enjoyable for you but could also help to prevent bullying!*

Making eye contact when you are talking to people, smiling and holding your head up and not slouching is very important as well, and will make you look confident! Also, if someone doesn't articulate or pronounce their words very well, it makes it hard to communicate with others and then it's easy to become isolated like Eric and be picked upon. Eric found that by performing magic his speech really improved, he spoke up and pronounced his words a lot better and as a result was more easily understood. And by being able to communicate better, more people were interested in what he had to say, he got more respect and he didn't get ignored like he used to anymore.

Speaking and communicating correctly is very important! That doesn't mean you have to speak with a plum in your mouth as they say. It doesn't matter what type of accent you have, but you should speak loud enough to be heard, pronounce your words clearly and not speak too quickly! This will also help to give you a look of confidence even if you don't feel it at the time.

People will judge you on how you come across to them. You see it's all about perception, the same as a magic trick, which is only an illusion. In other words, if you act like you are confident, then that's how people will perceive or judge you to be. It's a state of mind! Simple really, but it's true!

Also, the more confident you behave, the more confident you will become! In other words, you will get used to it and it will become second nature. So, practice at being confident the same as you would anything else! What you are doing is training your mind to think in *that way. And once you've convinced your mind you are confident, your actions will follow! But also remember that you don't have to be loud to be confident. You can be quietly confident, which is fine!*

CHAPTER SEVEN

THE MYSTERIOUS LETTER

Since becoming friends, Eric and Jack often met up and walked to school together, having a bit of banter with each other on the way.

"Where's your *girlfriend?*" said Jack, grinning.

"She's *not* my girlfriend Jack. How many more times do I have to tell you that?" replied Eric, grinning too as he shook his head. Jack changed the subject.

"So, where is Sheffield then?" Jack asked, knowing full well where Sheffield was all along.

"It's up north, of course!" replied Eric, surprised he didn't know.

"Oh yeah! I remember now ... Sheffield

United nil!" said Jack, unable to keep a straight face for very long before suddenly bursting out with laughing. Eric got the joke and joined in with the laughter.

There was no sign of the bullies on the way to or from school for most of the week, and during school time Eric only saw them occasionally. The bullies were keeping away now that Eric had made some new friends.

On Thursday morning all the children were sat at their school desks ready for their form teacher Mr Potter to call out the register. "So, what do you aspire to be when you grow up Jenkins?" asked the teacher.

"A computer software developer sir," answered the boy.

"A computer software developer, eh! Very good! And what about you Patterson?"

"I want to be a teacher like you, sir," replied a girl sat at the front.

"Good for you Charlotte ... Patel – what about you?"

"My parents told me that I am going to be a nuclear physicist sir! ... Or a doctor or a lawyer!" confidently answered one of the brainy students.

"Wow!" expressed the teacher, pleased. "... And what about you, Fartz?"

"A *magician* sir!" immediately replied Eric

without hesitation. There were a few pockets of laughter and sniggers heard around the classroom.

"Right, everybody, sit still and shut up or you'll get detention … Atkinson?" yelled Mr Potter as he started to call out the register.

"Here sir!" a boy at the back called out loudly.

"Brown?"

"Here sir," a girl at the front answered in a quietly spoken voice.

"Clarke?"

"Here sir!" called out another girl, eagerly raising her hand.

After calling out several other pupil's names, Mr Potter's finger moved down a line to the next name on the register. "Fartz?" Mr Potter called out to no reply. "… Fartz?" he repeated slightly irritated. "WAKE UP FARTZ! Are you daydreaming again?" Eric was a dreamer. Slightly startled, Eric's gaze immediately shifted from the window to Mr Potter's glaring eyes.

"Sorry! Here sir!" promptly replied Eric, now back into the land of reality, clearly feeling and looking tired after staying up late reading his magic book.

"Ah, you are alive!" said Mr Potter with his dry sense of humour to the sound of more laughter around the room. "Maybe I should have announced you as the wizard, or the magician, or perhaps the conjurer? I like wizard best! Have you got a *stage* name boy?" asked the eccentric Mr potter inquisitively.

"No sir, I haven't," replied Eric slightly puzzled, not quite sure where the questioning was going?

"Well, if you are going to perform magic Mr Fartz, then you are going to need a stage name. All the great magicians had one. Like 'Harry Houdini!'" Mr Potter told Eric as he paused from reading out the register.

"Whose 'Harry Houdini'?" asked Eric very interested to hear the answer.

"*Whose* 'Harry Houdini'! *Whose* 'Harry Houdini!'" Mr Potter repeated twice. "Call yourself a wizard and you don't know who 'Harry Houdini' was!" Mr Potter then said in a raised theatrical voice. "'Houdini' was only the *greatest* magician of all time, that's who!"

"But sir, I thought 'Merlin' was the greatest magician of all time?" responded Eric – Eric had read the story of the Arthurian legend 'Merlin the Wizard' many times.

"Ah, yes! But 'Merlin' is a mythological magician ..." answered the teacher.

"Oh!" just said Eric.

Mr Potter then went on to say, "One, can

even find the name 'Houdini' in the dictionary, symbolizing somebody who escapes from perilous danger! He performed at the turn of the twentieth century – that's the last century in case some of you *numbskulls* weren't aware!" added Mr Potter starting to calm down now. Mr Potter liked magic and even practised the magic arts himself in the past – and even had the stereotypical goatee beard to prove it!

"Did you go and see him perform *live* Mr Potter?" said a cheeky boy at the back to lots of laughter from the class.

"Watch it boy. I'm old but I'm not that old!" Mr Potter replied indignantly, trying desperately to maintain his composure, secretly thinking the remark was actually rather witty. "Right, everybody be quiet and let's continue or you'll *all* get detention!" he demanded as he glanced at his watch, realising the time. "… Johnson?" called out the teacher, raising his voice once again. And he then carried on calling out the rest of the thirty or more names, which made up the overcrowded class.

"Robinson?" called out the teacher, relieved to now be on names beginning with the letter 'R', thinking, "Almost done, and then I can get rid of this lot!"

"Here!" confidently replied Eric's friend, Jack Robinson from his slumped-out position.

"Here – *sir!*" bellowed Mr Potter, displeased.

"Sorry – here sir!" replied Jack, quickly sitting upright.

"Ryan ... *Emily* Ryan that is?" emphasized Mr Potter, as there were two pupils with the surname Ryan in the class.

"Yes, here sir!" called out Emily confidently. Eric couldn't help but stare at her admiringly from across the classroom.

As all the children were leaving the classroom, Mr Potter handed each of them a letter to take home to their parents. "Here you are, young man," he said as he handed one to Eric. "*So,* you fancy yourself as a bit of a *wizard,* do you Mr Fartz?

"Yes, sir," replied Eric enthusiastically.

"This might be of interest to you then?" said Mr Potter as he handed Eric the letter.

"Okay thanks, sir," replied Eric wondering what the letter was about?

"Shame you can't always *conjure* up your homework on time," dryly added Mr Potter almost cracking a smile.

"Carpe diem!" Mr Potter announced to the class, which was one of his favourite Latin saying's. *(Literally meaning: seize the day – in other words, make the most of it!)*

On the way to their lesson Jack said to Eric, "Old Mr Potter was really going off on one wasn't he about that famous magician ... what's his name? Larry Hou, Houd, Houdi." Jack couldn't remember his name.

" 'Harry Houdini!' " Eric reminded Jack, laughing. "I'll have to borrow my mum's laptop and check him out on 'Wikipedia'," thought Eric, keen to find out all about this famous magician.

"Mr Potters right though. You should have a stage name," said Jack as they both headed off to their first lesson of the day. Eric hadn't thought about that before.

All day long Eric wondered what the letter he was given could be about but didn't open it as it was addressed to his mum. What did Mr Potter mean by, "This might be of interest to you?" he pondered and then thought, "Oh I hope I'm not in trouble again!" and started to feel a mixture of worry and excitement all at the same time. He didn't remember getting another detention. "What could it be about?" he kept thinking. Eric couldn't wait to get home and learn all about 'Harry Houdini' and discover what this letter, which was driving him nuts, was about!

The bell sounded for home time and as Eric walked alone along one of the corridors on his way out of the building, he could hear loud music being played, coming from the music room up ahead on his left. Out of curiosity he peered through the music room door window and could see that it was a band rehearsing in there. He then quickly moved his head out of the way and crouched down on the floor by the door as he realised playing the drums was the bully David!

"What on *earth* are you doing down there?" said Miss Hopkins, one of the music teachers, who wanted to go into the room.

"Oh, I'm just tying up my shoelaces miss," replied Eric spontaneously, pretending to be tying them up.

"Off you go home now then, unless you are here to rehearse?" said the teacher.

"Rehearse? Rehearse for what?" Eric repeated in his head as he dashed through the reception area, accidentally knocking a bauble off the Christmas tree on his way out of the building.

He walked home by himself because his friend Jack had rugby practice straight after school. "At least if David's in there, he's not bullying me out here," thought Eric as he slowed down his pace and started to relax more. "But where is 'Hamburger'?" he then suddenly thought. He hadn't seen him in the music room. He told himself not to worry and carried on passed the row of shops on his way home. On the corner was the local 'Chippy' and just as he passed the entrance by a stroke of bad luck, 'Hamburger' was walking out the door stuffing his face with a double hamburger with cheese! They both looked at each in wide-eyed surprise!

"Oh 'eck!" yelped Eric as he made a run for it, his heart now beating fast with his school bag swinging back and forth across his back to the same beat.

'Hamburger' nearly choked on his hamburger as he tried to speak! "Oi! *Come* 'ere you!" he spluttered incoherently. His heart was beating even faster as he chased after Eric with his school bag doing the same motion on his back and with half a cheeseburger still in his mouth, some of it spilling out onto the pavement as he ran, with the other half still in his chubby right hand.

"You'll never catch me!" boasted Eric, feeling confident as he ran up one of the quieter side streets as fast as he could towards home, with 'Hamburger' several metres behind him in hot pursuit; the gap getting even greater with each stride! 'Hamburger' finished eating the bulk of what was still left in his big gob but was struggling to catch up – having big clumsy flat feet didn't help!

"Wait I just wanna *talk* to ya mate. *Wait!*" he yelled out to Eric in a less harsh voice now, panting and spitting the remains of his food as he spoke. Eric was having none of it and kept running as fast as his little legs could carry him, as he knew 'Hamburger' was just trying to trick him because he couldn't catch up with him. "You wait till I *get* you Fartz!" then angrily called out a red-faced 'Hamburger', now showing his true colours after realising that Eric was not going to stop.

Suddenly though, Eric lost his balance and went hurtling forwards, hitting the ground with a loud thud! *"Ouch!"* murmured Eric, shaken and slightly injured. Luckily for him, he held his arms out in front of him instinctively, which protected his face from the fall. But now there was no getting away. Just as Eric tried to get up, a sweaty, panting 'Hamburger' was now standing straddled over him, shirt un-tucked with his flabby belly flopped out, and with now just a tiny bit of the burger bun still left in his grip. 'Hamburger' gave Eric a pathetic kick to the ribs. Then stopped and crouched over with both hands resting on his knees and waited to catch his breath before continuing.

"Get on with it then. What are you waiting for?" muttered a sore and bewildered Eric, turning his neck around to look at him as he said it.

"Gimme me a *chance!*" replied a now even

redder faced 'Hamburger' still panting heavily with his sweat dripping onto Eric's face. Eric could smell his B.O even from where he lay!

"Call yourself a bully!" exclaimed Eric. It was a really weird conversation they were having.

"Bully? I've never called myself *'A bully'.* I'm not a bully!" snapped back 'Hamburger', not liked being called 'A bully'. *(Bullies or abusers never do and often they are in self-denial and won't admit to their problem. Eric's father never admitted to it either.)*

"Well what do you call this then?" argued Eric, hurting. 'Hamburger' couldn't give a reason or an answer to that. "If you punch me, I'll bleed all over ya!" Eric almost accepted his fate, but then heard the magicians voice in his head again. He managed to painfully turn over onto his back and just as 'Hamburger' was about to throw a punch at him. Eric held his palms out towards the bully in an attempt to stop him and quickly said, "I know *all* about you Gary!"

"What?" spat 'Hamburger' in an aggressive tone, pausing with his fist tightly clenched, poised just in front of Eric's defiant face, distracted by what Eric had just said. "No, you *don't!"* he added; sweat still pouring off him.

"I'm psychic and if you don't leave me alone, I will tell *everyone* about the pink furry slippers you like to wear!" threatened Eric.

"How on earth could he know that?" thought 'Hamburger'. He knew he could perform magic tricks, but this was a closely kept secret – or so he thought. *"What* pink furry slippers?" said 'Hamburger' acting in denial.

Eric sat up and put his fingers to his temples and went into a sort of a trance swaying his head as he did so. "Your mother's name is … Carol!" said Eric in a mysterious manner.

"What the …" 'Hamburger' said under his breath. He was starting to freak out and get scared. "You are just *guessing!"* he then said. "Okay, go on then, how many sisters have I got?" challenged 'Hamburger'. Unbeknownst to him, Eric knew all this information of course from the time he went over to his house!

"Two! You have two sisters!" answered Eric, releasing one of his hands from his temple to support his aching ribs. "One's named Abby and the others name is …"

"Stop!" demanded 'Hamburger', before Eric had a chance to name the other one. He didn't like it. Ever since a young child, he got easily frightened over weird and spooky things like that.

But Eric just continued. *"Mary!"*
"Stop! I said."

"You also have a dog named ... *Wait!* ... Kil–*la!* Don't you?" then stated Eric, really playing it up now, almost forgetting he was injured. He was starting to weirdly enjoy it, and this was his way of getting his own back.

"Please *stop it!* That's enough!" said 'Hamburger' with a slight quiver in his voice as he took a step backwards now visibly scared! "You're *weird!* Just stay away from me!" he then shouted as he ran away from the horizontal psychic as fast as he could.

Well, Eric had never seen 'Hamburger' run so fast and started laughing, but then quickly stopped as it hurt his ribs even more when he laughed. And as Eric lay on his back staring at the dark clouds above, he suddenly heard a sweet caring voice calling out, "Are you alright Eric?" A dark shadow then suddenly came over him. At first, he thought it might be an angel and that maybe he was dead, but then quickly realised he wasn't dead after all as his vision of dark clouds changed to a vision of beauty. Crouched over him was Emily Ryan trying to help him up, "Let me help you up," she said, concerned he was all right.

"Oh, *hi,* Emily! Thank you, but I'm okay. I just tripped over, that's all. I'll be all right," said Eric trying to act tough, but very pleased to see her.

"I saw that big *horrible* boy chasing after you from across the street," she said as she helped him up to his feet. Emily was the athletic type and a little bit taller than Eric.

"Oh, we were just having a race, that's all," responded Eric, not wanting her to know the truth.

"Well, it didn't look like that to *me*. You should tell your parents and report him to the school!" then said Emily in a forthright manner as she put her arm around his body to help support him as they slowly made their way down to the end of the road.

Eric just listened and then said, "... Actually, my parents split up, and I now live with just my mum."

"Oh! I didn't realise. Sorry to hear that!" said Emily thinking she'd said the wrong thing.

"That's alright. Anyway, tell me about you Emily. Where do you live?" said Eric quickly changing the subject.

"I live on the other side of Ramsgate in the Pegwell Bay area."

"Oh, the *posh* side!" quipped Eric. Emily just smiled. "You mean you came out of your way to help me!"

"I was just about to get the bus when I saw you looked like you were in trouble."

"That was very kind of you Emily," said Eric

thinking what a lovely and sweet girl she is – as well as being drop-dead gorgeous.

Emily and Eric had enjoyed chatting and getting to know each other a little better and reached the end of the road.

"Well, I'm very near home now. I only live over there," said Eric, pointing towards the housing estate. "I can manage from here."

"Are you sure you're going to be all right?" asked Emily as she removed her arm from around him.

"Yes, I'm fine, honest!" answered Eric with a big smile despite the pain he was feeling.

Emily leaned over and gave Eric a peck on the cheek. "See you tomorrow then, bye!" she said as she turned and walked back up the road she just came down.

"Tarra Emily!" called out Eric as he turned and headed in the other direction home.

Eric slowly managed to get back home, limping and crossing his arms to support his ribs as he did. His big winter coat had protected him somewhat and he was lucky to escape with just some bruised ribs and grazed knees.

Eric staggered into the flat with a huge grin on his face, still thinking about the kiss Emily gave him. As usual, he tossed his schoolbag down on the floor by the dining table, ready to do his homework. Only this time it was more of a drop rather than a toss.

"What are you *grinning* about?" asked his mum.

"Was *I?*" replied Eric, shrugging it off as if it was nothing.

"You're later than usual today love?" she said enquiringly.

"Yeah, I stopped and played football with Jack for a bit," he replied, lying to his mum once again. Although, he was tempted to tell her about him pretending to be a psychic and how the bully 'Hamburger' ran away from him scared!

"Did ya now?"

"Yeah!"

Quickly moving on to another subject, he said, "I've decided that now I want to be a magician when I grow up!"

"I thought the last time you said you wanted to be a policeman?" replied his mum, thinking he's forever changing his mind, and, whatever next.

"Well – I do – but I also want to be a magician."

"Take ya coat off and sit, down love," she said, suddenly concerned after noticing he was in some pain and finding it hard to stand up. She then fired a few questions at him. "Are you sure you're okay? You look a bit winded. You are not hurt, are you? You're not being bullied at school I hope?"

"No, I'm fine Mum, honest. I went in goal and just got hit with the ball a few times," said Eric reassuringly, still hurting but trying not to show it. "I'm glad she can't see all the cuts and bruises under my clothes!" he thought.

"Have you got any homework to do today?" asked his mum, checking to make sure. Eric was getting a bit neglectful about his homework lately.

Eric hesitated, thinking of saying, no. "Yes," he replied, deciding he would at least tell his mum the truth about that. "I'll do it later."

"Well, alright," she answered. "You just relax for now. Put the T.V on and I will go and make you a nice tea love." His mum cupped both her hands around his cheeks and kissed him affectionately on his mop of bright blonde hair. Eric then slouched further down on the settee and watched some TV. He was that tired he forgot all about the letter he was supposed to have given to her!

"After you've had your tea and done your homework, why don't you have a nice hot shower and then have an early night for a change, Son," said his mum seeing how tired he was.

"Yes, Mum," answered Eric, yawning.

After finishing his tea, Eric quickly got his homework done, but decided to forego having a shower and went straight to his bedroom. He got into his pyjamas and thought, "I must find out about that bloke 'Houdini'!" So, after climbing into bed, he went onto the 'Wikipedia' site, but fell fast asleep before he even had a chance to learn about the *famous* magician, 'Harry Houdini'.

Eric went to school the next day still feeling a bit sore, but the thought of Emily's kiss helped to take his mind off it. He was so lovestruck that he only washed one side of his face because he didn't want to clean the cheek Emily had kissed. And, because he couldn't stop thinking about her, he had once again forgotten about the mysterious letter which was still in his school bag!

It turned out to be a very enjoyable day for Eric for a change. He performed magic whenever and wherever he could, and got to know more about his new friends. And thankfully, he didn't have any problems from the bullies – David was too preoccupied with something else, and 'Hamburger' was too frightened to come anywhere near him! *(If you recognise in yourself that you are a bully, then try your hardest not to be, because you do have a choice: it's a matter of self-control!*

Maybe you have anger issues? Or maybe you are being pressurised into being like this by your so-called friends because that's how they act? Or maybe you too are a victim of bullying? It is recognised that bullying is often the result of the bullies having been bullied and abused themselves and they then take their own frustrations and anger out on other people.

Try to put yourself in the shoes of the victim; you wouldn't want to be treated in this way yourself! As the sayings go: 'You reap what you sow', and: 'What goes around comes around'. Meaning: how a person treats other people will determine how that person is treated eventually also – good or bad, positive or negative.

Being a bully and behaving badly will only lead you down a very negative and dark road and make your life miserable and unhappy as well! Nobody likes a bully and although you may think you have friends, the truth is probably the opposite, not real friends anyway. So, think about other people's feelings and be kind, and turn your negative energy into positive energy.

Taking up 'magic' as a hobby, for instance, will help you to focus on being positive. You will find that you can achieve great things by being positive and nice to people and live a much happier and more rewarding life!

If you are suffering from physical or mental abuse yourself and have anger issues, for whatever reason, and are struggling to deal with it; for your sake and those around you, seek help as soon as possible!)

CHAPTER EIGHT

NO TIME TO WASTE!

It was now the weekend, and on Saturday morning while Eric was outside playing football with Jack, his mum was hoovering his bedroom. And as she went to move his school bag, which he'd left open untidily in the middle of the floor, some of his books spewed halfway out and she noticed there was an crumpled up envelope sticking out between two of the books. Eric often forgot to give her the school letters. And, there had been quite a few recently regarding detention. "What's this letter about now?" she thought worryingly as she began to open it, thinking it was probably another warning letter to add to the pile.

As soon as she unfolded the A4 size letter, the title immediately put her mind at ease. It read:

'ST. BARTHOLOMEWS GOT TALENT!'

Then Ingrid saw the date of the competition, which was Friday the Thirteenth of December, and for a moment made her feel uneasy, sending a cold shiver running down her spine. 'Friday the Thirteenth' is supposed to be an unlucky day and the superstition apparently dates back many centuries! Ingrid thought it best not to worry Eric by telling him about it.

As Eric came back into the flat for his lunch, his mum said to him, "Who *forgot* to hand in a letter to me again, *young man?*" Holding the letter in question aloft as she said it. Eric suddenly remembered covering his hand over his mouth as it dawned on him.

"Oh, *sorry* Mum!" said Eric curious again to know what the letter was about.

"I'll give you *sorry*, this letter should have been given back into the school with an answer by the weekend!" said his mum in a jocular telling off sort of way.

"Given my answer in for what?" asked Eric, now even more curious.

"Your school is holding an end of term talent

to help pay the bill

"Oh, thank you very much, Mum!" said the delighted boy and gave his mum a big hug. His mum was pleased to do that as she knew what valuable experience it would be for her son to take part in the talent competition.

"I hope you are not too late to enter now though Eric," said his mum in a slightly concerned voice.

"Me too!" said Eric enthusiastically having now made up his mind he would go for it after all.

So, straight after Lunch with no time to waste Eric and his mum sat at the dining room table together with the laptop in front of them and Eric typed the domain name into the browser, and by some clever technological wizardry, the online magic shop website appeared!

"There's the magician we saw at the Christmas Fair!" said Eric pointing to a photograph of him on the website header. "Look at all the *magic tricks* they sell!"

There certainly were lots of different types magic tricks, from classic magic tricks to some of the very latest. And you could see photos and descriptions of the tricks, and even video demonstrations so you could watch the trick performed before deciding whether to buy.

All the various categories of magic were

listed in the menu bar. Eric was looking for 'Stage Magic Tricks'. "Ah, here they are!" he said excitedly, and clicked on the button. Eric then scrolled down the page as he started to look for magic trick products which he thought would be suitable to perform in the talent show.

"I'll leave you to choose a few tricks that you want, love. In the meantime, I must get on with the washing and ironing. Call me when you have decided, and I'll pay for them on my credit card," she said, smiling as she left.

"Okay, see you later Mum!" said Eric with his eyes still fixed to the laptop screen.

Eric continued the serious task of finding the tricks for his show. As per the letter the contestants only had five minutes max to perform – so he wouldn't need too many tricks. He remembered some of the performance advice the magician gave him at the magic stall. He had told him when putting together an act for a show, you need a beginning, middle and an end. You should start with a quick flashy trick to get everyone's attention and create interest, and during the middle of the act the tricks can be longer and more drawn out, but still be engaging to keep the audience attention. And the finale should be your most spectacular and impressive trick that people will remember!

Eric watched several magic trick video demonstrations and realised it was going to be hard to choose, as there were so many good ones he'd seen! The magician advised him to vary the type of tricks he performed so they weren't too samey. "Oh, what's this?" Eric thought. He watched as a magician poured himself a glass of 7UP, and while the liquid was still pouring, he let go of the glass and it remained suspended in mid-air! "That's amazing!" thought Eric and read the description and noticed that one of the bullet point's, claimed that it was 'Easy to do'! "That would be a fantastic opening trick!" decided Eric and promptly clicked on the buy button adding it to his shopping basket. He started to get very excited, thinking, "These tricks are really going to impress Emily!"

Eric then spotted the 'Change Bag' that he saw the magician at the magic stall demonstrate. He liked that trick as it was very entertaining and thought that would be a good one for him to perform. Eric, having a fun sense of humour also liked to make people laugh as well as amaze them when he performed magic. He remembered the magician telling him to always make the magic tricks entertaining! Also, you can do a lot of different tricks with it and it's nice and showy. So, Eric clicked on the buy button again and added the 'Change Bag' to his ethereal shopping basket. "Oh, I better have some 'Magicians Silk Handkerchiefs' as well!" he thought, so he added those as well.

Eric kept scrolling and then also saw the same comedy trick wand the magician at the magic stall had, which collapses when given to someone to hold. Eric thought, "I've got to have one of them!" and added it to his basket. Eric thought that was one of the funniest things he'd ever seen!

He found another trick called the 'Six Card Repeat', which he thought might be a good one to include and that was also added. He then saw another trick he liked, where a handkerchief changed colour as you pulled it through your hand, so promptly added that too. But he still hadn't found his closing trick!

"Haven't you finished looking yet?" asked his mum as she came back into the room.

"No, not yet. I'm still looking!" said Eric, with his eyes still glued to the screen. Then he saw a trick, titled, 'The Nest of Boxes'. "Um, this looks interesting," he thought, and started to read the description closely. The trick had all the ingredients for a good finale. It was showy and spectacular and seemed like an astonishing trick, but most importantly it would be very entertaining. The description said it was a classic of magic, where a borrowed finger ring wrapped in a handkerchief, vanishes and then after some comedy byplay, re-appears inside the smallest innermost padlocked box of four wooden nesting boxes, which are all tied shut with ribbons!

"Oh, I'd really like to perform that trick but it's a bit more expensive!" said Eric to his mum.

His mum looked at the cost at the checkout and said, "That's alright, Eric. I'll buy those tricks for you, but are you sure those are the ones you want?"

"I'm sure!" said Eric confidently. So, his kind mum paid for the goods and now all Eric had to do was wait for the parcel of wonder to arrive. Oh, and of course learn the tricks in time for the competition now less than one week away!

Eric was so excited! He couldn't wait to start learning his new tricks. He thanked his mum once again and went to his room to plan his show. He decided to go onto the 'Wikipedia' website learn about 'Harry Houdini'.

Eric discovered that they shared the same first name, as his real name was Erik Weisz and 'Harry Houdini' was a stage name. Eric also learned that 'Houdini' was born in Budapest, Hungary in 1874 and moved to the U.S as a young child. And as well as being a famous magician, 'Houdini' was even more famous as an escape artist, and escaped from a whole manner of restraints including handcuffs and chains, straitjackets while suspended from very tall buildings, and even police prison cells! He was a superstar of his day and became a legend, still talked about to this day! "Wow and he was a magician!" thought Eric totally engrossed in what he was reading.

But sadly 'Houdini' died an untimely death on Halloween 1926 when a stunt he performed went horribly wrong. Despite the doctor's advice, he refused to go to hospital as he was booked to perform at a sell-out theatre in Detroit, U.S.A, and being the true showman he was, believing in the old adage that 'The show must go on', ignored the advice and collapsed backstage at the end of the show. He was taken to hospital but sadly died a few days later from a ruptured appendix. A tragedy!

When Eric found out that 'Houdini' was a stage name, it reminded him that he needed a stage name as well. And, over the weekend as Eric also started to learn about other well-known magicians from the past, like 'Cardini' and 'Slydini'; he discovered that as well as

'Houdini', quite a few of them added the letters 'INI' to the end of their names too. So, Eric thought, *"That's it!* I will call myself *'Fartzini'!"*

Eric told his mum with great excitement and enthusiasm everything he'd learnt about 'Houdini' and other famous magicians whenever he saw her. And his mum really liked his stage name and told him, what a good choice!

On Monday Morning Eric met Jack as usual and they went to school together.

"I'm entering 'Bartholomew's Got Talent'!" said Eric enthusiastically.

"You're *brave!* I wouldn't have the confidence to do that! I'd be too nervous," replied Jack admiring Eric for having the guts to stand up and perform in front of lots of people. As although Jack was a very confident boy in normal everyday life, like a lot of people, he wasn't when it came to something like that! "Good for you!" Jack added patting Eric on the back.

Eric was quite surprised to hear Jack saying that and it made him think. *(Quite often, people who are 'shy' or are on the quiet side like Eric, like to perform, whether it's performing magic or something else. They do it not only because they enjoy it, but as a way of coming out of their shell to connect with people, and because of a desire to be liked and accepted! And if you are normally 'shy' and inward, then performing magic can be used as a bridge to connect with people and a vehicle to put over your personality.*

Lots of well-known stars of film and Television, theatre, and in the music industry, are quite shy! The confidence comes from being well versed at whatever it is you do and having gained enough experience to the point where you are self-assured at what you do! Now back to the story.)

As soon as Eric got to school, he ran up towards the school reception desk. "No running!" called out one of the teachers on their way to their classroom. Still, slightly out of breath, he eagerly handed over the even more crumpled up 'St Bartholomew's Got Talent' entrants form, confirming he would like to take part - desperately hoping it wasn't too late!

"You're a bit *late* handing this in, aren't you? This should really have been handed in by last Friday!" explained the very tall receptionist as she looked down at this diminutive figure at her desk. Eric was tempted to tell a porky again about his make-believe dog eating the original one but resisted.

"I'm sorry about that miss," said Eric with his fingers, and, his toes crossed.

"We've had a *lot* of interest in the competition this year and not everyone will be able to enter *otherwise* it will go on until *Midnight!*" stated the receptionist. She then asked inquisitively, "What is your talent then?"

"I am a *magician!*" Eric replied proudly.

"Oh, I don't think we've ever had a magician in our talent show before?" she announced trying to remember.

"May I borrow your pen, please?" he asked the receptionist. She handed Eric the pen she was holding, wondering what he needed it for. He removed the pen cap and held it in his closed left hand and announced, *"Watch! When I count to three the pen cap will disappear!"* Before she could protest, Eric started to count to three, and upon each count, tapped the pen, which substituted as a magic wand, against his hand. But as he went to tap it for the third time the receptionist's pen had disappeared instead of the cap!

The receptionist stood there speechless with her mouth open for a couple of seconds, then said, "Where's it gone?" Eric grinned and after a moment, turned his head and pointed towards his ear. The pen had reappeared behind his ear! "How on *earth* did it get there?" she thought, completely astonished.

"Let me try again," Eric said still grinning, knowing full well that the trick was supposed to happen like that. So, Eric once again counted to three, and much to the receptionist's further surprise and amazement, this time the pen cap did disappear! *(To learn this surprising trick called 'The Vanishing Pen Cap', go to the rear of the book!)*

"Wow! How did you *do* that?" asked the very befuddled receptionist, completely forgetting for a moment that she was there at work, not noticing that by now there was a queue of people behind Eric.

"It's *magic!"* said Eric as he returned the pen.

"That was amazing! What's your name?" she asked.

"Fartzini!" Eric replied.

"No, your real name, 'Silly Billy'," said the receptionist, chuckling.

"No, it's not Billy, miss!" innocently replied Eric. "It's Eric, Eric Fartz!" he then answered, a little confused having not heard that expression before.

"Are you having me on, young man. You should be a comedian!" then said the receptionist, her chuckle morphing into laughter. "... Well Eric, I hope that we will see you in the talent competition. All the entrant's names should be displayed on the notice board by home time today." Eric quickly thanked the receptionist, gave her one of his winning smiles and briskly walked away. *"... Hey young man,* what about my *pen cap?*" she called out. But Eric had already left, making his way to his classroom for another week of monotonous page turning. He would much rather be studying magic all day at 'Hogwarts', if a place such as this existed!

"Ah, *good morning* young wand wielder," said an upbeat, slightly wired Mr Potter – having drunk copious amounts of strong black coffee in the staff room – as Eric entered the classroom.

"... Oh, good morning sir," eventually answered Eric, who as per usual was in a bit of a daze.

"Well?" said the teacher inquisitively.

"Well what, sir?" replied Eric, clearly somewhere else!

"Are you going to be entering the talent competition?" asked his teacher, as if to say what else!

"Yes, I hope so sir, but I don't know yet? I have to wait to see if my names on the notice board," answered Eric as he sat down at his desk.

"Well, I do hope so too. I like to watch a bit of conjuring – I used to dabble in it a bit myself when I was a young man a Millennium ago. I like to try to figure out the *Modus Operandi!*" said Mr Potter buoyantly, even smiling on this occasion. Eric and the rest of the class looked at him bewildered? Once upon a time Mr Potter used to teach Latin and would suddenly come out with the odd Latin words every now and again. "It's Latin, meaning the methods for how the tricks are accomplished!" explained Mr Potter.

"Oh!" said the rest of the class all at once, even more convinced their teacher was from a different planet.

"Have you come up with a stage name yet?" then asked a curious Mr Potter.

"Yes, sir … Fartzini!" answered Eric in a quietly spoken voice. There were a few giggles around near where Eric was sat.

"I think that's a really cool name Eric!" said Emily standing up for him.

"*Class!* Will you *please* quieten down!" suddenly said the teacher as the noise in the classroom started to become increasingly louder.

"I took your advice sir and looked 'Houdini' up on the Internet, and that's how I came up with the name," said Eric more confidently and pleased to be talking about it.

"Well I also think that's a very good magicians name!" said Mr Potter.

"Thank you, sir," replied Eric, pleased.

"Is that 'The Amazing Fartzini' or just plain

'Fartzini'?" enquired his teacher smiling.

" 'The Amazing Fartzini' sir!" answered Eric proudly and confidently, smiling.

"Well, I hope it all goes well for you, young man!" said Mr Potter engrossed in the conversation and forgetting for a moment that he should have been calling out the register. "Okay, *quieten* down class – WHO THREW THAT ERASER?"

A lot of the topic of conversation amongst the class had been about the upcoming talent show. All day long Eric wondered anxiously whether his name would be on the list of entrants. He would pop by the notice board during every break, and even during class made the excuse that he needed to go to the toilet just so he could go and have a look. But alas, the list hadn't been put up, and Eric would have to wait now until home time to check. The anticipation was almost unbearable!

Eric never had any bother from the bullies that day either – David was far too busy rehearsing his band, desperately wanting to win the talent show, and 'Hamburger' was still too scared to go anywhere near him – not least because of Eric's threat of exposing his fondness for pink furry slippers.

There was still about three-quarters of an hour to go before home time, and in the school office, were the organisers of the talent show. The Deputy Head, the School Governor, and a couple of the teachers were still trying to decide whom they should select to be in it.

"What about Eric Fartz?" asked one of the teachers.

"Well, he's *very* late in entering! I don't think we will be able to fit him in now," said the School Governor.

"What does he perform?" replied the Deputy Head.

"He's down as a magic act?" answered the teacher looking at his form.

"Oh, a conjurer, eh! Well, we don't have a conjurer in the show, do we?" said the Deputy Head, mulling it over.

This year they had an unprecedented number of hopefuls enter, and so as not to make the show too long, limited the number to a maximum of twenty with each participant performing a five-minute. It may have had something to do with the fact they have raised the prize money to £100.00 for the winner this year. For the organisers, it was important to present a well-balanced show and try to pick the most talented and entertaining acts, because they would be representing the school.

The organisers finally made their decision, and with only about ten minutes to spare before the home bell was due to be rung, one of the staff members quickly ran around to pin up the list of entrants on the school notice board.

The bell sounded and loads of excited school children quickly rushed out of their classrooms, all heading in the same direction: the school notice board. It was almost like a stampede along the corridor with teachers and other staff members clinging on to the walls to avoid getting crushed!

"Good luck Eric!" Emily called out as Eric darted for the classroom door.

"Thanks!" Eric called back.

As Eric entered the packed reception area, he was immediately confronted with a lot of screaming and shouting with excited pupils barging and shoving one another in their quest to reach the notice board. It was very noisy – a mixture of joy and disappointment.

"Calm down, calm down!" yelled the Deputy Head in a commanding, authoritative voice from behind the safety of the reception desk.

As Eric got closer to the board, amidst the chaos, he could see the bully David bulldozing his way back through the crowd with a big smile and a re-assured look upon his face. "His band must be on the list?" thought Eric, still not knowing if his name was on there too.

There were still too many people in front of him to be able to see.

Eric finally got to the notice board where his eyes immediately started moving downwards from the top of the list, searching desperately for his name. And there it was, third from the bottom, 'Eric Fartz'! Eric was so delighted he jumped into the air with his arms above his head and screamed, "YES!" Anyone would have thought he'd won the competition already! Eric then quickly turned and ran out of the reception, smiling joyfully at the receptionist as he did, and ran all the way home with the smile never leaving his face. He couldn't wait to tell his mum the good news!

CHAPTER NINE

A DASTARDLY PLOT, A FALLING OUT, AND A SPECIAL PARCEL

"**M**um, Mum, I'm in the Talent show!" yelled Eric filled with joy and excitement as he came bounding into the house. His mum came through to greet him.

"Oh, I'm so glad to hear that, love," said his mum thrilled that her son made it into the school talent show. "I must remember to buy a ticket!" she suddenly thought, in a slightly panicked way. Then asked, "How many acts will be competing?"

"I think about fifty or so," replied Eric.

"*Wow!* That's a lot!" exclaimed his Mum surprised.

"Well it's a big school," said Eric as he removed his coat, hat and gloves, and his Sheffield United scarf, shivering slightly. It had been a particularly cold December's day. His mum had put some more money in the electric meter though, so at least the flat was nice and warm.

"Feels like it could snow," said his mum as she took his coat from him. "Wouldn't it be lovely if it snowed over Christmas, Eric!" she added, reminiscing about white Christmases when she was about Eric's age in Germany. "Oh, I do hope so!"

"Me too!" said Eric smiling widely at the thought of it.

You could tell Christmas was coming because Christmas cards had started to fall through the letterbox. "Oh yeah! A Christmas card arrived from your nan and grandpa in Germany," said his mum, suddenly remembering. Eric noted the German postmark, and happily ripped open the envelope, and gave the card to his mum to translate into English.

After doing his homework and finishing his tea, Eric went off to his magic den to continue planning his show, ready for the coming Friday. Eric was very excited at the thought of his parcel of magic tricks arriving anytime soon and tried to picture himself performing them.

Inspired by reading about 'Houdini's' many incredible escapes, Eric thought it would be a really good idea if he learnt an escape stunt himself. "This looks like a good escape to learn for my show," thought Eric as he found someone on YouTube, teaching an escape called, 'The Siberian Chain Escape'. *(Learn how to escape from a chain or a rope yourself! Find out the secret at the rear of the book!)* Eric watched the tutorial a few times and then went and fetched his old bicycle chain and padlock. He no longer had the bike just the chain and padlock. The bike got nicked in Sheffield a while back!

He soon realised that he couldn't tie his wrists up by himself and had to call his mum into his room to do it. And so, with his sleeves rolled up like his idol 'Houdini' as seen in the old magic posters, he practised escapology.

For the rest of the evening, his mum was in and out of his room tying him up by the wrists with the chain and padlock as instructed by her son. Every time he escaped; he would call her back in to tie him up again. Eric would roll around on the bedroom floor, grunting and groaning, trying to make his escape. Sometimes embarrassingly he couldn't get out and his mum would have to come and unlock the padlock to release him.

"You're getting *much* quicker!" said his mum who by now was desperate to have a cup of tea and relax on the sofa watching TV.

"Yes, I've got it down to about four minutes I think?" said Eric rubbing his now sore wrists.

"I think it's time you went to bed now Eric," then said his mum as she could see her son was tired and his wrists were a bit red. Plus he had school the next day.

"Can I just do it one more time please Mum!" said Eric, clearly tired and aching.

"No, it's time for your bed now Son," she replied more assertively. Eric would have gone on all night practising if he'd have been allowed!

"Okay, then Mum. Thank you for helping me. Goodnight!" said an exhausted Eric.

"Goodnight! Sleep tight!" his mum replied kissing her son on the head.

"Oh, Mum! Don't forget to watch out for the postman will you!" called out Eric as she started to leave the room.

"No, don't you worry, I won't forget! Night, night now," his mum replied as she pocked her head around the door.

"Night, night!" said Eric yawning.

The next morning arrived and the weather was much the same as the day before. Although, it looked like it had tried to snow during the night. Just before leaving to go to school Eric once again reminded his mum to keep an eye out for the postman so she didn't miss his precious parcel of wonderment being delivered. They were expecting a large parcel and it certainly wasn't going to fit through the letterbox!

"Bye, Mum!" said Eric, all excited.

"Bye! Mind how you go love. Don't worry I won't forget!" called out his mum reassuringly.

He met up with his friend Jack again on their usual route to school along the main road, passed the shops.

"Hiya Jack!" said Eric smiling

"Watcha Eric! What's up?" replied Jack, wrapping his coat tighter around him. "It's *freezing* isn't it mate!" said Jack, really feeling the cold and blowing into gloveless cupped hands.

"No, it's lovely and warm! What are you talking about? You southerners just aren't cut out for the cold," joked Eric teasing his friend for a change. They both laughed, stepping it out to get to school a bit quicker. Eric was cold too but didn't tell Jack. He was a proud northerner and hand a reputation to uphold.

Eric then announced in an upbeat sort of way. *"I'm* in the *talent competition,* Jack!"

"Oh, well done mate! You're gonna smash it!" said Jack, positively helping to boost his friend's confidence ahead of the competition on Friday night.

"D'ya think so?" said Eric being the self-doubting, and modest boy he was.

"Yeah!" Jack replied straight away.

"Ta, Jack," said Eric appreciating Jacks encouragement.

Just then Eric heard Emily's voice from across the road, "Eric, Jack!" she called out. Emily crossed the busy main road,

"Hi! Do you mind if I tag along with you to school?" asked Emily.

"If you want," said Jack feeling slightly awkward.

"Of course, you can Emily!" replied Eric very pleased to see her.

"It's *freezing* today isn't it," said a very rosy-cheeked Emily. Both boys nodded in agreement.

"Well look, guys, I'm going to dash on ahead," announced Jack feeling that three is a crowd.

"Yeah, alright, see you later pal!" called out Eric as Jack jogged on ahead of them.

"How are you now after your fall, Eric?" asked Emily caringly.

"Still a bit sore, but I'm doing good. *I'm* going to be entering the *talent competition!"* Eric answered and announced all in one breath, still excited by the thought.

"Oh, that is good news. I'm pleased for you. I am sure you'll do well – you are a really good magician!"

"Oh, cheers Emily," replied Eric moving closer to her as they walked.

"Call me Em, all my friends call me Em," she said smiling at Eric. "I never really liked magic until I saw you perform Eric. It's much better when you see it live rather than on the telly!" added Emily.

Just then Emily was about to walk under a ladder propped up against the wall of a shop building. Eric, acting instinctively quickly grabbed Emily's arm and pulled her away.

"It's unlucky to walk under a ladder!" Eric told her. But just as he said it, he accidentally tripped on a crack in the pavement. Both laughed.

"You're not superstitious, are you?" she replied, curious.

"No! Of course not!" said Eric denying it. Both continued to laugh at his funny mishap.

"Hey! I know a magic trick too!" suddenly said Emily, keen to show Eric the one trick she knew.

"*Cool!* I'd love to see it!" replied Eric.

Both stopped. Emily took a five-pound note out of her coat pocket, and then removed a couple of paper clips from her pencil case. Eric looked on curious.

"My grandfather taught me it!" said Emily as she folded the banknote into thirds and clipped the note together with the paper clips, clearly showing that the clips were well separated. She held the banknote between both hands and suddenly to Eric's surprise, snapped it open and somehow the two paper clips flew off and linked together in midair!

"Wow! That was *sick!* I've never come across that trick before?" said Eric genuinely impressed.

"Did you like it?" asked Emily pleased the trick had worked.

"Yeah! Will you teach me it?" asked Eric excited.

"Yeah, it's easy!" announced Emily and quickly showed Eric how to do it.

Meanwhile, while Eric and Emily were still walking and chatting on their way to school, David and 'Hamburger' were at their usual haunt in the children's play area, sitting on the roundabout plotting!

"No way, I'm *not* going to do it! Look, I don't want to be a part of it," 'Hamburger' told David feeling uncomfortable. 'Hamburger' wasn't the brightest of students, but he knew what David was planning to do to Eric was going a step too far! The conversation was by now starting to get heated and ugly.

"Don't be a *chicken!* Bruck, bruck, bruck," David responded, making a noise like a chicken as he moved his arms up and down like a pair of wings.

"You could get *expelled* for that. No, *forget* it!" said a defiant slightly nervous 'Hamburger'.

"*Don't* be a *scaredy* cat, it will be a laugh Hamburger, go on," said David still trying to coax 'Hamburger' into something he clearly didn't want to do.

"No, not this time mate," 'Hamburger' said shaking his head as he unwrapped a toffee.

"What's gotten into you? You've *changed!*" David questioned 'Hamburger'.

"I just don't want to do it anymore. Besides, if you're *so* confident that your band will *easily* win the competition, then you don't need to worry about Fartz being in it, do ya!" said a wiser than usual 'Hamburger' trying to evade being involved with David's dastardly plot.

David laughed, "What? *I'm* not worried about *him* being in it. *Don't* be silly! What makes you say that? He's got *no* chance against my band – we're *much* better than he is!" snapped back David in an arrogant and cocky manner. They had noticed the amazing reactions that Eric was getting, and it made David jealous and even angrier towards Eric. "... Actually, come to think of it, I've noticed you seem to have been avoiding Fartz lately!"

"He *knows* things! He's one of those, um ... psychics or whatever ya call em!" exclaimed 'Hamburger', finding comfort eating his toffee.

"What *things?*"

"Nothing," said 'Hamburger' as he got off the roundabout and started to walk away, not wanting to talk about it.

"What, are you *scared* of him or something?" David called out to 'Hamburger', laughing. "You are scared of him, aren't you? And that's why you won't do it!" David made a noise like a chicken again. "Bruck, bruck, bruck. I'm gonna call you *Chicken* Burger from now on!"

"No, *of course* not!" replied 'Hamburger' as he continued to walk, and now starting to feel a little bit of what's it's like to be on the receiving end for a change.

"Get *lost* then! I'll do it on my own, I don't need you – *loser!*" David angrily called out to 'Hamburger', who was now walking with his back to him some distance ahead. "FATSO!"

'Hamburger' had his private reasons to keep out of Eric's way, but after hearing David's cruel and evil plan, he thought it was best to cut all ties with him.

David was used to getting his own way. He

came from a well-off family and was a spoilt brat, always getting what he wanted whenever he wanted it. His father David Snr was a successful businessman who owned several businesses in the area. And his mum, Penelope, was a lady of leisure. They lived in a wealthy part of Ramsgate, called the Westcliff, in a four-bedroom executive home and had flashy cars and so on, and liked to show off their wealth. His father also happened to be the School Governor and had some influence over how the school was run.

All day at school Eric kept thinking about his parcel arriving and couldn't wait to get home and open it and start learning all the new tricks. During class, he would daydream – thinking about performing his magic show in the talent competition and imagine himself winning. There was a real buzz in the air with lots of groups of pupils discussing it and who they thought might win.

Eric was sat at his desk in a history lesson with five agonising minutes still left to go until home time – his eyes flitting back and forth between the clock on the wall and his open textbook showing a picture of Henry VIII seemingly smirking at him – eagerly waiting for the home bell to ring out its joyous sound.

Time seemed to drag on. At one point it

seemed to Eric that the hands on the clock were moving backwards!

"The time won't go any quicker by you staring at the clock, young man," said Mr Potter to Eric, looking over his spectacles and raising his bushy eyebrows.

"10 – 9 – 8 - 7 – 6 – 5 – 4 – 3 – 2 - 1!" Eric counted down the seconds in his head, but the bell didn't ring. Eric's face dropped, then a minute or so later the bell did ring, and all the children jumped straight up out of their seats, bags swinging over their shoulders as they scrambled for the door. "Why is the bell *always* late rather than early?" thought Eric as he picked up his bag and joined the rush.

"Hold up! Hold Up!" yelled the teacher. The children froze in their positions. *"Who* said you lot could go? I didn't say you could go. The bell is *not* there to tell you that you can go, the bell is there to tell *me* to tell you that you can go! Okay, *off* you go!" said Mr Potter, showing who ruled in his class.

Eric sprinted home again for another day on the trot, buzzing with excitement and anticipation at the thought of discovering the secrets that would behold him once he opened the parcel.

"Mum, I'm *Home!* Has it arrived?" Eric called out excitedly as he opened the front door.

had a quick look inside the box to make sure the other tricks he ordered were there, still buzzing with excitement.

"Thank you so much, Mum!" Eric said to his mum delighted.

"You are welcome Son," she replied, smiling.

"I had better start learning all this magic now!" said Eric, realising the urgency.

"Yes, love ... *Oh!* By the way, I went to one of the local charity shops and bought you a nice black tailcoat and bow tie. And I even managed to find you a top hat, although it may be a little on the large size," commented his mum as she picked up his coat from the floor and started clearing away the ripped up pieces of paper discarded all over the place. "... You can try your costume on later love. I can always adjust things if need be?"

"Great! Ta Mum," said Eric, feeling slightly overwhelmed by it all. Eric didn't know what to start learning first. He opened one of the products and started reading the instructions as he carried all his new magic props to his bedroom to start learning them in time for the talent show, which was now only in a few days!

CHAPTER TEN

THE RUGBY GAME

The next morning Eric struggled to get out of bed, still feeling tired after staying up late practising his magic act. His mum had to call him umpteen times before he finally got out of bed and got ready for school. On his way out of the door, he suddenly remembered it was the 'Lower School Inter-House Rugby Tournament' that afternoon and quickly dashed back inside and grabbed his rugby gear with a feeling of dread.

Eric hated rugby, as apart from the fact he wasn't the physical type, he knew that David and 'Hamburger' would be playing on the opposing team.

So, with his heavy bag of schoolbooks over one shoulder, his PE kit over the other, and his dirty rugby boots tied together by the laces around his neck, which he neglected to clean from a week ago, off he finally went to school.

Jack was already waiting for him on the corner with his schoolbag and PE kit over his shoulders also. But his rugby boots were spotlessly clean! Jack took his rugby very seriously and played for the school team, usually in fly-half position, and couldn't wait to get out onto the sports field and play his favourite sport. Both boys were in St. Georges house.

"Look at the *state* of your boots!" laughed Jack. "Mr Jones is gonna to give you a *right* telling off if he sees them like that!" stated Jack shaking his head in bewilderment. Eric wasn't really listening and just grinned, as he had other things on his mind. Namely, magic and Emily.

Mr Jones was their PE teacher. He was from The Valleys in South Wales and spoke with a thick Welsh accent and was passionate about rugby. He was a big tall strapping fellow who once played at a professional level as a lock. Eric didn't like him because he was always shouting and telling him off and would always make the boys have showers even if the water was cold. Mr Jones was very OCD with the rules when it came to rugby.

"The weather has improved a bit today. The grounds still a bit hard, but we should still be able to play!" commented Jack enthusiastically.

"We?" laughed Eric. "I *never* get to play a game! I'm rubbish anyway and can never remember the rules!" piped up Eric, self mockingly, his mind now focusing on the conversation Jack was trying to start about the rugby tournament today.

"Well, I'm the team captain – so *I* get to pick the team! I'll see if I can get you a game today Eric," said Jack reassuringly as they now both headed for school.

"The house will only lose if you pick me Jack!" replied Eric half-jokingly. So far Eric had always been a substitute, which he didn't mind at all and would rather Jack didn't pick him.

Jack noticed Eric kept looking across the road, probably looking for Emily, "Hey, have you asked Emily out yet?" he asked, being nosy and now changing the subject. Eric ignored the question, "Go on tell me –"

"Mind your own business! We're just friends!" replied Eric wishing Emily and he were more than just friends.

"Yeah, *sure* you are. Don't be a melt! Why don't you just ask her out, you know you want to?" said Jack with a huge grin. Eric didn't answer, just smiled and shook his head at his friend's persistence to find out the truth. "Look do you want me to ask her out for ya?"

"No, *I don't!* I can do it myself," responded Eric, realising he had just spilt the beans.

"*Oh,* so you do admit you fancy her then!" said Jack with an even bigger grin.

"Is it that obvious?" said Eric, finally admitting it.

"*Err,* yeah!" replied Jack nodding as if to say you can't-fool me this time.

"She kissed me the other day!" Eric suddenly announced, smiling.

"*What!* She *actually* kissed you. *Shut up!*" said Jack, surprised and slightly jealous as Emily was probably the prettiest girl in the class.

"Yes! she did!" said Eric with an even bigger smile.

"Yeah, *sure* she did?" questioned Jack not believing it.

"Don't believe me then," said Eric still smiling.

"Straight up?" asked Jack.

"Straight up!" replied Eric.

"You *lucky* thing!" said Jack now starting to believe Eric.

"I suppose I am," thought Eric as they both walked through the school entrance grinning at one another.

In the afternoon, all the Lower School pupils headed towards the sports field for the rugby tournament. The usual racket was heard much to the annoyance of teachers in nearby classrooms trying to teach. The house rugby teams made their way to the changing rooms, whilst the pupils not taking part lined the pitch ready to support their house teams. The changing rooms were in the sports block in the shabby-looking old part of the school, adjacent to the sports field.

The groundsman had done a fine job at giving all the lines on the rugby pitch a fresh coat of white paint in readiness for the tournament. And Mr Jones, the sports teacher, had already finished inspecting it and was now keen to start. He was kitted out wearing his Welsh national rugby shirt, which he wore with pride, white shorts, spotlessly clean rugby boots, and his whistle, which he kept attached to a piece of string around his neck. "What on *earth* is taking the players so long?" he thought, getting impatient waiting for them.

In the boys changing room Eric was showing Jack and some of the other boys some magic tricks. "Lend me your tie, Jack," asked Eric.

So, Jack picked up his crumpled-up tie from the bench where he had just tossed it. "There ya go," said Jack as he handed Eric his tie keen to see a magic trick. Eric then proceeded to tie a knot in the centre. Pupils looked on wondering what Eric was going to do.

"Now watch!" said Eric, raising his voice to be heard above the din of noise in the testosterone and bravado-filled room. He blew on the knot, and to everyone's amazement, the knot dissolved away! *(Learn this quick and astonishing trick called 'The Magic Knot' at the rear of the book!)*

"Wait! What? Do that again!" said Jack and turned to one of his mates saying, "Did you see that?" Pupils shook their heads in disbelief.

There was one boy sat on the bench nearby listening to music through his earphones.

"Can I borrow your earphones a minute pal?" asked Eric loudly to him. The boy didn't hear him very well at first and took one of the earpieces out and said "What?" Eric repeated his request as Jack and the others encouraged the boy to do so. What for? The boy said, unsure about what was going to happen to his precious earphones.

"He's gonna do another trick!" said Jack still trying to work out the last trick. The boy then cautiously handed them over to Eric.

"You better not ruin them," the boy said as he watched Eric produce a pair of scissors from his school bag.

David and 'Hamburger' were at the other end of the changing rooms with the rest of the St. David's house team, but purposely sat apart from each other as they were no longer friends. David could be heard from the other end of the room, bragging as usual about how good he was at rugby to anyone who cared to listen, and how they were going to thrash all the other teams! The normal rivalry you get between schoolhouses. He wasn't the captain of his house rugby team but liked to think he was.

The three other house teams were doing the same, taunting each other as they were getting changed and putting on their rugby boots. Not the majority of Eric's house team though. They were watching him about to cut a pair of expensive earphone wires in half!

"Look, you can clearly see the wires have been cut in half!" exclaimed Eric after he cut them to everyone's surprise and shock, especially the boy who lent them. "Now Watch!" He tucked the ends of cut wire into his fist and then rubbed the two ends together with the fingers of both hands." The tension built and then Eric quickly moved his hands out of the way to show the earphone wires were now completely restored! *(Discover the secret to this remarkable trick called 'The Cut and Restored*

Earphones' at the rear of the book!)

Jack and Eric bumped fists together and all those that could see what just happened applauded and praised Eric. Eric then handed back the earphones to the much-relieved boy who checked that they were indeed working again. "That was well cool!" he said and then carried on listening to his music.

David noticed it was Eric getting the applause, which he hated and was now even more determined to follow through with his dastardly plot on the night of the Talent competition!

"What's all this commotion going on in hear then!" shouted Mr Jones in his strong Welsh accent as he came bounding into the changing room carrying his all-important clipboard. "Quieten down! Come on you lot, you should have been on the pitch by now! Come on hurry up, hurry up!" He stood by the doorway studying the boy's rugby boots closely as they passed him on their way outside. He was a real stickler for having clean boots and having the studs securely tightened.

Eric had still not cleaned his filthy boots and tried to hide behind some of the bigger boys as they went out. He thought he'd got away with it as he walked past the stern looking teacher. But then he heard, "Fartz! Come here, Boyo!"

Eric knew then that he was in for it!

"Sorry sir," said Eric before the teacher had even told him why he had stopped him.

"They make those boots in black as well you know," said a displeased and annoyed Mr Jones sarcastically as he looked down at Eric's brown muddy boots, shaking his head. Eric kept his head lowered and didn't dare argue. He'd seen boys do that before and regretted it because they then had their punishment doubled. "Right, once around the field, off you go Fartz!" demanded the stern PE teacher. "And, no dawdling!"

Before long there were other boys who also hadn't learnt their lessons joining him running around the large sports field. Some boys would be very disappointed at missing out on the rugby games, but to Eric, it was the lesser of the two evils. Eric also saw it as a good opportunity to go over his magic act and purposely ran slowly. And it wasn't long before the other boys had already caught up with him and were now in front of him.

The rest of the rugby teams were now on the pitch doing warm-ups and throwing the practice balls back and forth to each other. Jack was one of the first on there, keen as ever. Mr Jones blew his whistle loudly and shouted out to everyone in his booming voice to gather

head of his, he was yelling and cheering, "YES! FANTASTIC! WELL DONE ST. DAVID'S!"

During the playoffs for the 3rd or 4th position, Jack made a couple of substitutions, and gathered his team around him to talk tactics. Jack knew the next game against St. David's was going to be even harder as they were up against some very good school rugby team players as well as two huge boys, known for their dirty tactics, David and 'Hamburger'. Eric was very relieved that he remained a sub.

The game finished with St. Patrick's house team coming out the victor, placing them in third place.

After a short interval, Eric watched on from the touchline as his friend Jack and his team swapped places with the losing team ready to play in the final against St. David's. Even before all the players got into position there was some unpleasant taunting going on between the two teams, started by big mouth David of course.

"Hurry up into your positions lads. We haven't got all day!" said Mr Jones impatiently as he ran with the ball towards the halfway line.

The weather had warmed up a bit and the sun even appeared out from behind a cloud occasionally. It was ideal weather for a rugby game as the ground had by now softened somewhat, which lessened the chances of players becoming injured and breaking bones as they fall.

All the houses made a wall of sound around the pitch as they chanted for their house teams. This was a chance for the winning team to gain some valuable house points and both teams were determined to win!

"Come on St. Georges!" shouted Eric along with the rest of his house. Emily was with her girlfriends in a group further along the line. Occasionally Eric and Emily would catch each other's eye smiling at one another.

The ref blew his whistle for the start of the last game of the afternoon, the final, and Jack kicked the ball high well into the opponent's half. Both teams were rested by now and were abound with energy as they darted for the ball hoping it would be their team who put the first number on the scoreboard. The ball landed with a bounce and was caught by one of the opposition players, who ran forwards with it several metres before passing it behind him to his team-mate, who then made some more ground as he passed it to 'Hamburger', the ball spinning through the air as it travelled. But 'Hamburger' decided not to pass it as he'd been taught, but instead selfishly run forwards with it looking for glory, bulldozing his way through his opponents. He managed to barge his way through a couple of players and reach the opponents 20-metre line while dragging a player along with him who was still clinging on to his legs. But 'Hamburger' was then finally tackled to the ground with a loud thud.

Eric gave a big cheer upon seeing him fall over, thinking back to about a week ago when he was the one doing the falling-over.

As 'Hamburger' landed, the ball fell out of his grasp causing him to lose possession as the scrum-half from the St Georges team quickly picked up the ball to cheers from his house. He then ran forwards passing it backwards along the newly formed line, continually moving forwards unchallenged and making good ground as they did.

As they reached the 5-metre line, the ball was past to the winger who found open space and sprinted to the try line, running right around behind their opponent's goalposts before touching the ball down to the ground.

"Come on! What are you playing at? Get it together!" David shouted angrily at the other forwards, assuming the unauthorised role as captain.

St. Georges had made a good start. Now it was up to the fly-half, Jack, to put the ball between the posts. The ball was placed into position on the ground carefully on its end and Jack stepped back several paces ready for his run-up. There was silence in the air, apart from a few taunts for him to miss, from the other house. Jack paused holding his nerve and then ran and kicked the ball. The ball soared through the air and over the crossbar to loud cheers again from his house.

"GET IN! ... GET OVER THERE!" Eric screamed loudly, suddenly remembering it wasn't football and quickly changing what he was saying mid flow not to look stupid. But it still didn't come out right. He looked around slightly embarrassed to see if anyone, especially Emily, had noticed and carried on cheering as the players got back into their starting positions.

"That boy down there keeps looking at you!" said Georgina, one of Emily's friends pointing towards Eric.

"What boy? replied Emily knowing full well whom she meant.

"The blonde-haired boy who does magic tricks," described Georgina.

"Really!" she replied, not letting onto her friend that she secretly had a crush on him.

"He's actually quite cute," remarked her friend.

following it as it made an arch and started it's decent. Jack acted quickly and made a dash for it catching it in his arms and cradling it like a precious newborn baby.

He crossed the twenty-metre line with it and just before he was grappled by the ankles and brought crashing down to the unforgiving ground, he threw the ball back to one of his players, who in turn threw it to the winger. The winger then sprinted with lightning speed down the wing as everyone in the St. George's house came closer to the touchline and loudly cheered him on as he ran past them. No one was going to be able to catch this boy. He was the fastest runner in the year! Was this going to be their opportunity to equalize?

The winger who had played in both the games suddenly developed a cramp in his legs and collapsed to the ground in agony accidentally dropping the ball forwards. The whistle blew for a scrum awarded in favour of St. David's team, but as the ref and linesman got nearer, they soon realised that the boy was not going to be able to carry on and needed assistance. The boy was helped off the pitch by the PE teaching assistant and applauded as he left. "What a shame!" thought the St. Georges house team and supporters. They may not get this chance again.

So now Jack had a dilemma. His fastest player was now off the pitch and he needed to make a substitution. Did he bring on one of the larger boys who weren't very fast but have played before or did he risk bringing Eric on who had never played an actual game before and by his own admission was 'Rubbish'. "Eric was very fast at running though," thought Jack. He'd certainly had plenty of experience and practice at that recently by being chased by the bullies! So, much to Eric's horror and surprise, Jack called him over as a matter of urgency, "You're up Eric!" and he was no longer a sub, but now a player.

There were only another three minutes left to play! Eric came running on overshadowed by all the other larger boys around him.

"If you get the ball, just run as fast as you can along the wing and touch it down over the try line!" said Jack secretly to Eric, covering his hand over his mouth as he said it. Eric nodded and adopted his position as winger. *"Come on lads* we can do it!" shouted the very determined Jack. The tension was very high!

"Form a scrum!" The ref shouted to the forwards. "Quick as you can now boys!"

As David passed Eric to join the scrum, he nudged him on purpose and quietly but menacingly threatened him, "I'll get you now try and get the truth out of him. "You will tell me if you're being bullied won't you, Son"

"No! *I mean,* yes! Stop asking me that – I've already told you I'm not! Don't *worry* Mum," said Eric as he leaned away from her slightly irritated.

His mum was all too aware of a period of bullying her son went through at his previous school in Sheffield. She stepped in back then and made the school aware of it straight away, and they dealt with it. *(If you are being bullied, it is always best to tell your family and people in authority straight away – nip it in the bud as they say, so it doesn't continue! Don't suffer in silence like Eric!)*

Eric got a bit gloomy and upset. "I'm not going to be able to enter the talent competition *now!*"

Ingrid tried to reassure her son by saying, "Luckily for you, you haven't broken any bones! The swelling will come down by tomorrow. You'll have a big bruise and it will be sore still for a few days, but your hand should be okay by Friday evening my darling."

Eric's mum used to work as a nurse back in Sheffield. She chose not to work locally as a nurse because she didn't want her ex to find out where they were now living, and she knew that hospitals would be the first place he'd search.

" 'Houdini' wouldn't have let something like this stop him performing, would he now!" said his mum, encouraging her son to not get despondent and give up.

"Your right Mum!" replied Eric, thinking about his hero. Eric felt much happier after hearing his mum say all that. Buzzing with excitement again, he then told her all about the rugby game. Telling her once again how fast he ran with the ball as the whole house cheered him on! And, that his friend Jack scored a try and won the game with a dropkick!

"I have got your favourite dessert for you after tea Eric!" said his mum with a big smile on her face.

"Apple Strudel and ice cream!" Eric called out very pleased.

"Yes!" replied his mum pleased that Eric was happy again.

After his tea and a second helping of dessert, Eric decided to go to his room to rehearse his act ready for Friday. He had learnt the tricks and what to say but he just needed to polish up his act. Luckily the swelling had come down a lot and he was able to move his hand quite freely, although it was still sore.

Ingrid could hear her son rehearsing in his room. "I went to see a magician the other day, and he performed this amazing card trick where he counted one – two – three – four – five – six cards. He then threw away one – two – three cards. But to everyone's amazement, when he counted the cards again, lo and behold he still had one – two – three – four – five – six cards!" said Eric, reciting his patter as he performed the trick, throwing the cards all over his bed.

"Don't overdo it love, will you? Your hand needs to rest!" called out his mum.

"I won't, I'll just practise for a bit longer that's all!" replied Eric from the other side of the door, keen to get it right.

CHAPTER ELEVEN

A SURPRISE VISITOR

Thursday morning at around 10:45 am, Eric was at school and Ingrid was at work serving at the checkout.

"Good morning madam," said Ingrid to a customer.

"That accents not from around here?" said an elderly lady placing her shopping onto the conveyor belt. "Where are you from? No don't tell me, let me guess … somewhere in Yorkshire, am I right?"

"Yes, top marks," said Ingrid as she scanned a tin of cat food. "I'm from Sheffield."

"I have a small bed and breakfast in Nelson Crescent, near the harbour. We used to get a lot of tourists from all over, not so much now mind you, but you get to recognize the various accents after a while.

"I'm sure you do –" said Ingrid, suddenly distracted by a commotion going on nearby in the frozen food's aisle. "Somebody, call, an ambulance!" screamed one woman. A crowd was gathering and as Ingrid stood up, she could just about see someone lying on the floor not moving. Ingrid immediately asked a colleague to take over and ran over to help. "Move out of the way please, move out of the way. I'm a trained nurse! Give me some space!" announced Ingrid. Ingrid acted without thinking and did what she was trained to do.

It was a large man probably in his sixties. He had collapsed possibly with a heart attack still holding a frozen pizza in his hand! She removed his scarf and unzipped his winter coat. He was wearing a smart suit and tie, so she undone his top shirt button and loosened his tie to make sure he hadn't just fainted or slipped and hit his head. She took his pulse and said, "Can ya hear me, love?" But she was unable to make the poor fellow come around, so without hesitation, she tilted his head back and performed CPR on him as the crowd looked on in dread.

After a few attempts, it worked! The man

soon opened his eyes, totally bewildered to what had just happened. Soon after that, the ambulance arrived, and the medics took over. Luckily, he was okay and was wheeled out to the ambulance. The medics said that if it hadn't been for Ingrid's quick response it could have been a different story! Everyone was full of praise for her and the man's wife couldn't thank her enough.

"I didn't know you were a nurse?" said her friend Carol who was on the checkout next to her, surprised and impressed. "Aren't you a *'dark horse'* then!"

"You were *amazing!*" called out another checkout girl.

"Okay *girls,* the drama is over, less of the chatting and back to work please, we have a store to run," said the business-minded duty manager.

"*Alright!* Keep ya *hair* on!" Carol answered back, being cheeky.

"And, somebody, please *pick* that pizza up for Pete's shake in case somebody *slips* over on it!" the duty manager then said panicking, not wanting any more incidents that day.

In the afternoon, Ingrid, as usual, walked home from her shift at the supermarket, avoiding the cracks in the pavement as she did, feeling very pleased that she had been able to help potentially save somebody's life.

She arrived home to be greeted outside her flat by a photographer snapping pictures of her and a zealous young local newspaper reporter keen to get her story.

"Hello! Mrs Fartz?" questioned the reporter as Ingrid was trying to open the front door.

"Who's asking?" asked Ingrid inquisitively, always suspicious of any strangers!

"My name is Sally and I work for the local 'Gazette' newspaper and we would like to feature your story of how you saved The Mayor of Ramsgate's life today!"

"The Mayor!" thought Ingrid, surprised. "… Oh, I don't think so love," said Ingrid. Then humbly, "I don't want a fuss made of me. I just did what anybody else would do in those circumstances."

"Lots of people have been contacting the paper and saying what a *heroine* you are, and the local community would *love* to hear all about it Mrs Fartz."

"Well …"

"It is *Mrs Fartz,* isn't it, and not Mss? Where is your husband, is he at work?"

"Erm," just muttered Ingrid.

"You're not from around here, are you. Have you just arrived in the area?" asked the reporter continuingly firing lots of questions at Ingrid, which she didn't want to answer.

Ingrid then quickly stepped inside the flat and shut the door on them, leaning her back against the door suddenly starting to panic. The letterbox then opened, and the reporter's slightly annoying voice could be heard again. "If there are any questions that you don't want to answer, that's fine Mrs Fartz you don't have to answer them. We just want about five or ten minutes of your time, that's all! I shan't ask too many questions … *Mrs Fartz?*"

During the momentary silence, Ingrid mulled it over carefully. "Well, if they are going to print this story anyway, I had better make sure they have all the correct facts – besides it's only for a local newspaper." So, she reluctantly opened the door and let them in to do the interview. She also secretly quite liked the attention.

"Okay, please come in. I have never done this sort of thing before," she said, feeling butterflies in her stomach.

"Don't *you* worry Mrs Fartz, we'll be in and out of here before you know it!" stated the reporter as she stepped over the threshold.

"Would you like a cup of tea?" asked Ingrid politely.

"Yes, milk with no sugar please," said the reporter as she got her notepad out.

"Milk and two sugars please," then said the photographer.

Ingrid brought the drinks into the lounge. "I hope I've got these the right way around?" she said slightly overwhelmed by the whole thing.

"Just *smile* for the camera!" said the photographer in a blasé done this a million times sort of way.

"I haven't done my *hair!*" said Ingrid feeling self-conscious as she ruffled her long black hair with blonde roots.

"I understand you are a nurse?" asked the reporter smiling and poised ready to write down every word.

"Used to be. I *used* to be a nurse," replied Ingrid giving only brief answers.

"That's a northern accent, isn't it? Where are you from originally?" inquired the reporter after taking a sip of tea.

"Sheffield," answered Ingrid reluctantly, not wanting to give too many details away.

"Oh, *Sheffield!* That's a *long* way away!" then commented the reporter. "What brings you down here then?" the reporter added trying to appear friendly. Ingrid didn't answer that question. The reporter then noticed a photo framed picture of Eric on the mantelpiece and after a slightly awkward pause, asked Ingrid, "Oh, *who's* that? Is that your son?" asked a determined reporter trying to get as much information as possible out of her.

"I thought you said you weren't going to ask too many questions," said Ingrid abruptly and sounding very guarded.

"Sorry! Sure, no problem. Now, Mrs Fartz. In your own words, please go ahead and tell us what happened!"

The reporter wrote down everything Ingrid told her, and another pot of tea and one hour and fifteen minutes later they finally headed out the door. "Oh, *look* at the time! Doesn't time *fly!*" said the reporter looking at her watch. "There should still be time for your story to go to print before the deadline and make it into the 'Gazette' tomorrow!" added the very pleased looking reporter having got her story. "Thank you very much Mrs Fartz, goodbye!"

"Thanks for the tea!" called out the photographer as they left.

"Tarra!" replied Ingrid as she shut the door behind them, relieved that it was over. She felt very tired and weary after all the questioning.

Ingrid had said more than she would have liked to about herself and her family, but thought, "What's done is done now," and shrugged it off thinking no more of it. Ingrid then set to work making some alterations to her son's stage costume, adding a shiny silver ribbon trim around the lapels of the tailcoat ready for tomorrow night.

At the school that day, the main topics of conversation were the rugby tournament and the upcoming talent competition. The tickets for the show had completely sold out and the school organisers were very busy still preparing for it. There was certainly a lot of excitement in the air at St. Bartholomew's and especially because the school was breaking up for the Christmas holidays the following week. The pupils were finding it very hard to concentrate on their school subjects, which was normally the case for Eric anyway but even more so this week. All he could think about was the talent show!

Eric's mum was right, the swelling had gone down completely by the next day and apart from the obvious sign of a bruise and some slight pain still, his hand was functioning as normal, much to their relief. Eric even managed to perform a few card tricks during the breaks, which he had learnt from his book with a normal pack of cards, and once again amazed pupils and staff with his spellbinding magic! *(Go to the rear of the book to learn some of Eric's favourite card tricks with a normal pack of cards!)*

And so, after a day of thinking of nothing

much else but magic, Eric made his way home from school pleased at the thought that he'd been able to perform magic and would be able to enter the talent competition after all.

Meanwhile, in a small B&B guesthouse in Ramsgate, a tired, slightly unkempt looking man, wearing dark sunglasses was checking in at the reception desk.

"Please fill in your details on this form if you would sir," said the old landlady to her guest, feeling slightly uneasy in the stranger's presence, not being able to make eye contact with him.

"Tah love," said the stranger as he picked up the pen. Finally sliding his glasses up onto his forehead, revealing his piecing steely blue eyes.

"Long Journey?" she then asked, shooing away her meowing, over-familiar tubby black cat as it brushed itself against the slightly irritated stranger's leg one last time.

"Aye!" he just replied not wishing to get into a conversation.

"Will you only be wanting to stay the one night? Only we do have availability if you wish to extend your stay?" inquired the landlady smiling, hoping to get more business.

"Aye, just the one night will do for now, maybe more if need be?" he replied invasively, keen to get to his room and rest. He quickly filled in the form and handed it over.

"Okay, here is your room key Mr Smith. Breakfast is from 8 am till 9 am. I hope you have an enjoyable stay with us!" said the landlady handing over the keys. The stranger took the keys and carrying just a sports type bag, went upstairs to his room.

"I'm *home,* Mum!" called out Eric as he slung his school bag down in the tiny hallway and removed his coat and hat before entering the living room.

"I'm on the *phone* love!" said his mum in a quiet voice as she covered the mouthpiece with her hand. "... Sorry Julie, please carry on." Ingrid smiled at her son and indicated wouldn't be, long.

"I was just saying — typical of me to have a day off when on the rare occasion there's some drama at work," said Ingrid's friend, finishing what she started saying.

"I *couldn't* believe it, Julie, when I heard it was the *Mayor of Ramsgate!"*

"What, you didn't know who he was? asked Julie, slightly surprised.

"No! I didn't have a *clue!"* replied Ingrid, eyebrows raised.

"Didn't that big gold chain around his neck give you a clue then?" quipped Julie making light of the situation.

"No, he didn't have a chain around his neck!" said Ingrid, chuckling at Julie's wicked sense of humour. "You are terrible you are Julie –"

"What's that about the Mayor, Mum?" interrupted Eric, overhearing the conversation.

"Julie, I've got to now, Eric's home!"

"Okay, thanks for calling me and letting me know. I will look out for the 'Gazette' tomorrow," quickly said Julie. "Wish Eric good luck from me for tomorrow night, bye!"

"Will do, see you tomorrow at work. Bye!" said Ingrid as she put the phone down. "Hello, Love! How are you – how's your hand?" asked his mum, still not come down to earth quite from everything that had happened earlier.

"My hand's fine, but what was that about the mayor?" asked Eric keen to find out.

"Tell you what love, I'll make us a nice cuppa tea and I will tell you all about it!" she said as she got up to go to the kitchen. She then started singing.

Eric promptly shoved his headphones into his ears, turned up the volume on his favourite playlist, and got out his cards and started practising a 'Riffle Shuffle', 'Card Fanning', and even attempted a 'One Handed Cut', while he waited, curious to know what had happened.

"Here we are love, a nice cup of tea for ya," said his mum as she sat down to tell her son all about what happened. Eric listened to his mum telling him all about saving the Mayor of Ramsgate's life and about the interview she had with the local 'Gazette' newspaper and felt very proud of her.

Later on, his mum helped him move the dining room table over to one side, and wearing the stage costume his mum had put together for him, Eric performed the complete act from beginning to end in front of her, adding the final touches to it. Eric's mum was very impressed by how his magic act had come on, giving him lots of applause with high hopes for her son doing well in the talent show.

"I wish Dad could see me perform my magic act," said Eric as he packed his magic props away.

"Yes, but you know that's not going to be possible darling," replied his Mum, being realistic.

"I suppose not," then said Eric looking a little disappointed.

At the guesthouse the next morning at 8 am on the dot, the stranger was sat down at the only setup breakfast table, alone in the slightly musty smelling room ready for his breakfast.

"Your early for breakfast, guests aren't normally this early?" said the old landlady as she came in. "I trust you slept well?" The stranger didn't reply. "Would you like beans or tomatoes with your breakfast?"

"Beans, ta love," replied the stranger of few words, who was looking out the window towards the sea, occasionally hearing the muffled sounds of seagulls squawking.

"Tea or coffee?" she then asked.

"Oh, tea, please – hey, I don't suppose you've seen this woman and this boy before, have ya?" enquired the stranger, showing her a small photo of what looked like him several years younger, together with a woman and a young boy, both with blonde hair with his arms around them.

The landlady took the photo from him and looked more closely. "No, sorry I can't say I have, " she said shaking her head, although, she thought the woman's face did look familiar. Curious, she then asked, "Why?"

"Don't worry," said the stranger curtly, seeming slightly on edge as he snatched back the photo and shoved it back in his wallet. The landlady then went to fetch his breakfast …

"Here you are dear," said the landlady as she placed his plate of food down in front of him. "You're from up north, aren't you?" she asked, trying to be friendly. The stranger confirmed he was with just a nod and half a smile. "Whereabouts?"

at 9 am. He couldn't see Ingrid among them, and it had now started to rain and the visibility through the windscreen was poor. As he waited and listened to the monotonous sound of his windscreen wipers and the amplified raindrops hitting his car roof, his thoughts turned to the grim reason why he was there!

It was the day of the talent show and Ingrid kissed her son goodbye as he went off to school and she hurried off to work slightly late with her umbrella over her head dodging the puddles.

After about fifteen minutes or so had passed, Peter suddenly noticed a group of women come around the corner of the building, but because they all had umbrella's open obscuring his view, he couldn't see if his ex was among them. The three women entered the store to be greeted by the duty manager not looking very pleased.

"*And* what time do you *call* this then ladies?" sarcastically said the manager to them. It was Ingrid, Carol and Julie arriving slightly late for work.

"Sorry!" they all said as they quickly headed for the staff changing room chatting away as they did.

"*Hurry up then!* These are not self-service tills!" called out the manager hurrying them along as he looked at his watch.

"I saw you in the paper," said Carol walking behind Ingrid and Julie.

"Yeah me too, you're now a celebrity in this area!" added Julie, both thrilled their friend got recognition for what she did.

Ingrid smiled saying, *"Celebrity?"* Ingrid laughed. "I'm hardly a celebrity!" Thinking as she said it, "I'm just glad the newspaper only has a small circulation and my ex won't read about it up in Sheffield!" Little did she know he was parked outside waiting for her.

It was now two minutes to nine and the three checkout girls sat at their checkouts adorned in their uniforms ready for a busy Friday shift. The car park by this time had started to fill with customers – waiting in their cars until the last minute so as not to get wet – poised ready for the store doors to open.

Peter leaned his head forward to get a better view as he now noticed more women had sat down at the tills and scanned his head along the row of tills looking for a dark-haired woman that resembled his ex-girlfriend. Then he saw someone that he thought might be her on the end till. So, at 9 am when the store doors opened, he casually walked into the store, still wearing his 'Ray-Bans', and blended in with all the others, pretending to be a shopper.

He got to the aisle on the far side that led down to where Ingrid was sat. He needed to get closer to her though to be sure it was her but didn't want to get too close in case she saw him. So, he walked down the aisle – disappointingly, not the wedding ceremony aisle he had once hoped for – trying his best to be inconspicuous, slightly distracted by all the bottles of booze he could see lined up along the way tempting him to buy. He then stopped, pretended to look at what was on the shelves, and then leaned back and made a quick glance over towards her. He then quickly leaned forward again so he was out of her sight, turned and walked briskly away and out of the store. Peter had found who he came looking for!

He went and sat back in his car waiting for her to finish work, as he wanted to confront her somewhere private and alone like a predator waits for the right time to strike its prey! So, he waited and waited, sat put in his car staring intently at the store's entrance not wanting to miss her leave.

At 2 pm Ingrid and her friend, Carol finally finished their part-time shifts and left the supermarket together. It was still pouring with rain as they started to make their way home together, umbrellas aloft, merrily chatting to one another.

Peter's body suddenly jerked forwards, his eyes widening as he spotted them leave. He then stealthily got out of his car and started to follow them. Walking some twenty metres behind them, soaking wet and concealing something in his hand hidden behind his back. After a while, he suddenly stopped as they stopped!

"Bye Ingrid!" said Carol.

"Bye Carol ... Oh! Are you coming tonight?" asked Ingrid referring to the talent show.

"Yes, and Gary's coming too! Surprisingly I didn't even have to coax him into it? It will make a nice change for him, rather than being stuck in his bedroom playing video games all evening killing zombies!" replied Carol raising her eyebrows. Ingrid agreed, nodding her head. "Anyway, *must* go, wish Eric good luck from me. *Bye!*"

"Tarra love, mind how you go!" said Ingrid, adding, "Remember its Friday The Thirteenth *today!*" Both chuckled, and after saying their goodbyes yet again one last final time, they parted company and Ingrid walked the rest of the way home alone – or at least, so she thought!

Peter continued to follow her all the way to where she now lived. Ingrid opened the door, shaking her umbrella before closing it, really feeling the cold, and went inside. She put the kettle on and went to get changed.

She'd just got changed and there was a knock, knock at the door. "Who could that be? It was a bit late for the postman?" Ingrid thought as she made her way out of her bedroom and into the hall. "Oh, it's probably another newspaper reporter again or maybe a T.V reporter this time!" she convinced herself as she flung open the door unusually unguardedly. But it wasn't a reporter; it was Ingrid's ex and father of her son standing there dripping wet! Fear immediately spread all over her body as she suddenly realised, who it was!

"Hiya love!" he said as he started to remove his suspiciously shielded hand from behind his back. Ingrid screamed loudly fearing the worst and immediately slammed the door shut on him! He always told her jokingly that he would kill her if she left him, but was he really joking? "I'm not gonna *harm* ya lass! I just want to talk ta ya, that's all!" Peter called out from the other side of the door – his voice, now slightly muffled.

"Go away or I'll call the *police!*" Ingrid shouted back frightened, her heart pounding.

"I miss you both and I had to find you. Can't we just talk things through? Ingrid, *please, we need* to talk!" he pleaded, the rain still pouring down.

Ingrid didn't answer and kept silent. She then pulled the net curtains aside a little and peeped through the window to see the surprise visitor. There he was, holding a now sorry-looking bunch of somewhat wilted flowers – her favourite, Carnations. Ingrid couldn't help but laugh and let out a big sigh of relief, feeling slightly silly that she had screamed like she had over some flowers.

Peter continued talking to the door. "I've changed Ingrid! *Honest,* I 'ave! I've stopped the drinking and I'm getting help. I haven't touched a drop for about a month … any road I'm *really* sorry for all the heartache I've caused you and Eric … I love you!"

He had apologized, which she knew never came easy for him and Ingrid could see he was genuinely upset and remorseful. He then stopped talking and with his head dropped down, he turned and started to walk away. Then the door opened.

"Aren't those for me?" said Ingrid, feeling somewhat emotional, more reassured now for her safety as she invited her wet and bedraggled but still handsome ex-boyfriend into her new home and back into her life, albeit temporarily. "You can't stay long. Eric will be home from school in about an hour or so and seeing you here out of the blue like this would be very unsettling for him – *I mean it,* Peter!" she said assertively, still feeling slightly shocked and unsettled to see him *herself.* This was her new home now, and she wanted to make it clear that she was only allowing him in under her terms. "Your right we do need to talk, come in, and take those *ridiculous* sunglasses off!" She shook her head grinning, unsure whether she was doing the right thing.

He walked into the tiny flat, compared to where they once lived together, his shoes making a squelching sound as he did and handed her the flowers – both smiling, both hurting inside.

"You look *beautiful* Ingrid … even with dyed black hair!" said her ex, jokingly, referring to her new incognito look. Peter preferred her hair blonde.

"Do *I,* are you sure?" replied Ingrid, flattered but unconvinced as she caught a glimpse of herself passing by the mirror on the wall as she hung up his wet coat.

"What were thee screaming for ya *daft* thing, anyone would think I was trying to *kill* ya!" said her ex, chuckling and trying to make light of the situation, pleased to be allowed in. There was no hugs or kisses, but both were secretly pleased to see one another.

She handed him a towel to dry himself, made them both a cup of tea and they sat down to talk. "I've stopped drinking and I've straightened my life out now," he repeated, but the odd whiff of alcohol on his breath betrayed his otherwise believable claim — she didn't comment.

She basically told her ex, trying not to get too emotional, that both her and Eric had now moved on with their lives and were happy living down in Ramsgate. She told him that they had both made close new friends and that Eric had settled down now at his new school, and that she was not ready to move back together with him, at least not for the time being.

Peter, of course, found it painful to hear as he had hoped that they would be together as a family once again in Sheffield, and one day maybe even marry. But he told her he understood why they had left him, especially after everything he'd put them through. And he was pleased that they were both happy. Still trying to come to terms with it, he reconciled himself by thinking, "At least she's not closing the door completely on our relationship and there's still a chance we could get back together in the future!"

Ingrid was very pleased to hear he was trying

to conquer his drink addiction and praised him for that. "He did seem to have improved a little. And who knows," she thought, "maybe he would become a changed man?" She still loved him, but it was going to take time for the wounds to heel.

"I'd really like to see our son before I leave to go back to Sheffield. Even if it's from a distance!" said Peter, his eyes starting to well up, showing his rare emotional side, desperate to see him again.

Ingrid then told Peter all about Eric's new hobby and how passionate he was about performing magic, and how it had really helped to make him a lot more confident. She then went on to tell him that Eric was going to be performing his magic act in the school talent show that very evening.

"The show is at St. Bartholomew's C of E School in Ramsgate and starts at 7.30 pm. Come along and poke your head in at the back of the audience and watch him perform!" said Ingrid trying her best to make a compromise.

"Thanks for telling me that Ingrid," he replied smiling, very pleased he would be able to see his son at last.

"Peter, it's time for you to leave now as it won't be long before Eric gets home!" Ingrid then said slightly panicking having seen what the time was. They both got up and Ingrid went and opened the front door for him. "Ah, the rain has stopped!"

"Please pass on my love to our son, won't you?" said Peter as he put on his coat, still damp from the rain.

"Aye, *of course,* I will Peter!" she replied, but at the same time thinking, "When the time is right!" not wanting to build up Eric's hopes too soon of his mum and dad getting back together again in case it didn't work out.

"It's been lovely to see ya, Petal!" Petal is the name he fondly used to call her. "Please keep in touch, the house is empty without you both!" Teary-eyed, he then stepped out the front door, sad to be leaving.

"Yes, okay. Take care driving back to Sheffield! Tarra Peter!" replied Ingrid full of mixed emotions, slightly sad he was leaving, both desperately holding back the tears. Part of her still belonged to Sheffield.

"Aye, I will. Tarra!" They did embrace one another this time, both pleased to have cleared the air somewhat. And then after wistfully staring into her eyes one last time, Peter turned around and this time walked out of her life!

CHAPTER TWELVE

THE TALENT COMPETITION
FIRST HALF

It had been a normal school day at St Bartholomew's. However, there was great excitement and anticipation in the air from Pupils and teachers alike in the build-up to the talent show taking place that very evening. A lot of organising and preparation had gone into putting it all together and the day was finally here. The school assembly hall was the venue; it could hold up to four hundred people and all the tickets were now sold out! It was a large stage with plenty of space backstage in the wings and behind the twinkling starlight curtain for the multitude of acts to store all their musical instruments and props and to prepare themselves before going on stage.

It was a real variety show with lots of different types of acts taking part, including singers, musicians, dancers, a comedian, and a magician! The hall had been decked out with Christmas decorations and in the corner, by the stage, there was a large beautifully decorated Christmas tree with lots of empty boxes of different shapes and sizes covered in shiny paper and tied with ribbons pretending to be Christmas presents under it. On the other side there was a very old, out of tune, upright piano, which if it could talk would probably moan and say something like, "Please play some modern tunes rather than boring old hymns for a change!" The chairs were all stacked around the hall ready to be placed into position in neat rows by the volunteers before the guests arrived.

At school closing time Eric and Jack were chatting by the school entrance gates waiting for Emily. Eric had arranged to meet Emily there so they could walk home together again.

"Ah, there's Emily over there! I'm going to get going then, Eric. *Good luck* tonight mate!" said Jack to his friend, patting him on the arm.

"Thanks, pal, see ya later!" replied Eric acting cool as the two friends bumped shoulders.

"Ask her *out* this time!" Jack reminded him as

he sprinted off. Eric smiled and chuckled at Jack's continued attempts at matchmaking and picked up his school bag.

"... Hiya Em!" said Eric as Emily came over to meet him.

"Good, you remembered to call me *'Em'.* Hi, how are you?" said Emily smiling.

"Fine thanks, you?" replied Eric smiling back but acting a bit vacant.

"I'm grand, thanks. I hate it when it gets dark this early, don't you?" asked Emily to no immediate reply.

"... Sorry, what?" then said Eric, distracted.

"I said – oh, nevermind – are you looking for someone?" she then asked, noticing Eric seemed a little apprehensive, looking over his shoulder occasionally.

Eric shook his head. "No, no, shall we go then?" he replied. In fact, he was checking to see if the two bullies were about, but he couldn't see them anywhere, which made him feel more relaxed.

He never spoke about the bullying to Emily either. Especially not to her, because apart from the embarrassment associated with it, he thought she might think less of him and probably wouldn't want to hang around with him anymore. In fact, he never really wanted to admit it was happening to him, himself! *(It is*

quite normal to think in this way. You can rest assured,
most people wouldn't think less of you, and would be
sympathetic and want to help you. In fact, they would
think you are brave for speaking out. So never be
worried or feel too ashamed and embarrassed to tell your
family and friends and people in authority if you are
being bullied. As the old saying goes, "A problem
shared is a problem halved!")

The rain had now stopped, and Eric walked with Emily to her bus stop so she could get the bus home to Pegwell Bay, sidestepping the swimming pool like puddles as they went. He wanted to hold her hand but wasn't sure if she liked him in the same way.

"My bus should be along any minute?" said Emily as they joined the queue.

"That's alright, I'll wait here with you," replied Eric, wanting desperately to ask her out, but now felt even more nervous than when he performed his first magic show. So, instead, he asked, "... D'ya wanna – see an amazing magic trick?"

"Yeah, sure I'd *love* to! As long as it's not another *card trick!*" joked Emily. Eric had already shown her lots of card tricks during the school breaks. *(It's always best not to perform too many of the same type of tricks or make your performance too long, or it could become boring!)*

"I promise Em," said Eric with a nervous

laugh, hesitating as he tried to pluck up enough courage to ask her to be his girlfriend.

"... Well, *hurry* up and get on with it then before the arrives!"

"Okay, okay," he replied. Then, when he felt he'd built up enough courage, said, "D'ya wanna ... chocolate?"

"Yes please, I love chocolates!" answered Emily delighted at the thought.

Eric searched his pockets, but then said with a slight grin, "Oh, I'm sorry Em, I thought I had one left, but I must have eaten it!" Emily just laughed, still waiting to see this amazing trick, he said he'd show her. Eric then removed his mobile phone from his pocket, opened his photo gallery app and showed her a photo of a chocolate, about the same size as a real one. "Look, I took a photo of it."

Emily looked at him as if he'd gone bonkers or something and started giggling. "Is this a wind up?"

He then said, "Of course if I was a *real* magician, I would be able to remove the chocolate from the screen!" Eric paused for just a moment and then did just that! It looked astonishing as he appeared to remove the chocolate from right out of the screen, leaving an empty space where the photo was a moment ago, and hand Emily a real, 3D chocolate!

(Learn how to do this amazing Twenty-First-Century trick at the rear of the book!)

Emma stepped back in amazement. *"What? That was amazing!* That *can't* be?" she screamed in delight "You're like a *real-life* Harry Potter!" Emily couldn't believe it and started to sniff the chocolate as if to check if it was real, slightly unsure. "Well it smells real!"

Eric laughed. "Go on eat it then," he said with a big grin.

So, Emily popped the chocolate straight into her mouth. "Um, it tastes real too!" she said. Though, Emily still couldn't quite believe it was real even as she joyfully munched away on it. It even seemed to taste better than normal. "… Um, yummy!" she said with a big smile on her face. "Thank you, that was really *sweet* of you! … *Sweet* of you, d'ya get it?" repeated Emily as she nudged Eric. "Oh, forget it."

Eric then laughed having finally got the joke. He'd been too transfixed staring into Emily's eyes to notice she had cracked a joke. He had got the love bug all right!

"It's very dark without that streetlight on!" Someone announced as more people joined the queue, forcing Eric and Emily even closer together. They both then looked into each other's eyes and smiled.

"I really like you Eric!" said Emily quietly

spoken.

"I feel the same way about you too!" replied Eric feeling more confident.

"Don't make yourself late for the competition," she then said changing the subject. Both felt slightly awkward in this situation.

"I won't," said Eric letting his bag drop to the ground as he stood on his tiptoes so he could be the same height as Emily.

"Oh, I really hope you win tonight, Eric!" Then, upon saying that they both spontaneously closed their eyes and pursed their lips, about to kiss. Suddenly the bus pulled up, over a big puddle, splashing everyone. Both opened their eyes and retracted their heads before they had a chance to kiss.

"See you at the show later!" said Emily as she moved away from him and stepped onto the bus.

"Bye Em!" Eric stepped to one side to let the others behind him, past, feeling slightly disappointed. The two of them then waved goodbye to each other through the bus window as it left.

Eric couldn't believe his luck, even though he didn't get the chance to kiss Emily. "The prettiest girl in the class actually fancies me!" he thought. He ran across the road, jumping in as many puddles as he could, and then all the way home with a big happy smile on his face, feeling chuffed with himself. He thought to himself, that even if he didn't do well in the talent competition, nothing could put a dampener on his day now!

Eric arrived home from school having just missed his dad unbeknownst to him by about ten minutes or so.

"Hi Mum, I'm *home!*" called out Eric as he came bounding in through the kitchen door and kicked off his soaking wet shoes, immediately holding his nose and pulling a face, saying, "Ergh!" upon noticing the unmistakable strong smell of bleach in the air.

"I'm in *here!*" she answered back. His mum was in her bedroom busy removing stuff she'd kept stored away inside a large beaten-up old suitcase so that Eric could put all his magic props inside to carry to school. Whilst she was doing this, she came across a few old holiday snaps of the three of them smiling happily together as a family, which instantly brought a smile to her face. As she reminisced, she thought, "If only it could have carried on being that way!" Just then Eric burst into the room making her jump.

"*Hiya!* You look like you've seen a *ghost!* Are you alright, Mum?" said Eric.

"Hiya! Yes, you just startled me that's all – I was miles away," replied his mum thinking, "Maybe I *did* see a ghost?" Certainly, a ghost from her past! "Take this suitcase into your room Eric and start packing all your magic props ready for the show, and I'll go and put your tea on."

"Okay, ta mum," said Eric as he picked up the suitcase.

"This is the only suitcase we have large enough I'm afraid," she said, noticing one of the wheels was missing.

"Hey! I *thought* there was something *different* about you. I've just noticed your hair is *blonde* again – I wondered what that horrible smell was!" exclaimed Eric, having only just realized and now curious as to why she had decided to change back to her old look. "How come then?"

"Well, I just fancied a change – and besides, I don't think we need to worry about anyone knowing where we live anymore," she answered. His mum had been referring to his dad of course. "Anyroad, we need to hurry up!"

"Yeah, okay Mum," he replied as he headed straight to his room carrying the suitcase.

"Don't take too long now will you, we don't want to be late!" she called out as she headed for the kitchen, her hair still slightly wet, starting to panic a little bit.

Eric took the empty suitcase into his room and packed all his magic props inside, double-checking he hadn't forgotten anything. Lastly, laying his black tailcoat and his bow tie on top of everything. He could only just about shut the suitcase! He certainly couldn't fit his top hat into it, as it wasn't one of those collapsible types. He was going to have to either carry it in the other hand or wear it. "I'll carry it!" he thought, laughing to himself at the prospect of him wearing it into school. Suddenly his mobile beeped, it was a text from Emily. It read: 'Good luck for tonight x.' Eric replied to say thanks, also putting a kiss.

The contestants had to be at the school hall half an hour before the show started to have a sound check and get ready. So straight after tea, Eric and his mum closeted themselves in their warm winter coats, scarves, gloves and woolly hats and set off for the talent competition, struggling with the large heavy suitcase of magic paraphernalia between them. On the way out, Eric quickly grabbed an orange from the fruit bowl and put it in his pocket; his mum was pleasantly surprised to see that Eric had chosen fruit to eat for a change.

It was very cold and dark outside by now and some of the streetlights were out on their estate. As they looked up into the clear night's sky, they could see a myriad of twinkling stars and there was a full moon out. It certainly was a very magical night indeed.

When they finally arrived, having had to stop a few times to have a break from carrying the heavier than usual suitcase, they were confronted with a very noisy and chaotic scene, to say the least. The show organizers were running around like headless chickens trying to sort out some last-minute hitches. There was a singer on stage having technical sound difficulties, while lots of other contestants and their families were milling about everywhere, not quite sure where to go!

"Ah! 'The Amazing Fartzini'!" called out Mr Potter, who had volunteered to help.

"Good evening, sir," replied Eric as they approached him.

"Please find a space backstage to put your things. Here is the running order for the show," he said, handing Eric a sheet of paper.

"Thank you, sir," said Eric, starting to feel a bit overwhelmed by it all. He noticed that he wasn't on until the second half.

"Remember to keep your 'Secreta', 'Secreto'! And as they say in the theatre – 'Break a leg'!"

"Break a leg! That's not very nice!" Eric thought as they made their way backstage.

('Break a leg' is an old theatre saying, meaning, good luck.)

Eric was now starting to feel the pressure. "Mum, when you're nervous, why do they call it 'Butterflies'?" enquired Eric.

"Well, it's because you feel like there are lots of butterflies dancing around in your tummy tickling you. You just need to wave your magic wand and make them all disappear Eric!" said his mum reassuringly. "It's known as stage fright, love, and it's quite normal to feel in this way." She then added, "You'll be great, Son!" And the two of them went to join the other nervous acts and unsavory smells backstage. *(Having the right mindset when it comes to dealing with pressure, really helps. So, use pressure as a positive thing rather than a negative thing!)*

Eric placed the suitcase down on the floor by some scenery from a previous school production of the 'Lion King'. Then unzipped it and started to remove his costume and magic props. His mum helped him by hanging his tailcoat on a costume rail nearby, while he neatly set up the props on a small round table he had borrowed, covered with a shiny black cloth with silver stars, which his mum had made for him. The 'Nest of Boxes' took up so much space there was hardly any room for anything else!

Eric had decided not to perform the 'Siberian Chain Escape' after all because he didn't want to take the risk of possibly running over his allotted time and being disqualified, or even more embarrassingly, not being able to escape at all.

As Eric prepared for his magic act, there were also lots of other contestant's backstage preparing for their acts also. Some of the singers were warming up their vocal cords, while the dancers were seen to be stretching their limbs, doing the splits, and one girl lifted her leg right up next to her ear! "That looks painful!" thought Eric grimacing. A violinist was tuning her violin, a trumpet player was blowing into his trumpet, and a comedian was quickly pacing up and down reciting his jokes, making Eric feel a bit dizzy just watching him.

On stage just finishing their sound check was David's band, a heavy metal band calling themselves 'The Zombies', who were down to close the show. They had put zombie make up on, gelled their hair up, and even ripped their clothes to shreds, looking quite scary as they thrashed out a 'Black Sabbath' number very loudly. David didn't need to put makeup on to be scary. He looked like a cross between a zombie and 'The Joker' villain out of 'Batman'. By contrast, Eric put on his smart tails coat and black bow tie keen to get ready.

"You're getting ready very early love?" said his mum as she adjusted his bow tie for him. "Look at me – *that's* better."

"Alright Mum *stop fussing!*" said Eric, feeling slightly embarrassed by his mum.

"Well, you want to look *smart,* don't you?" she responded, giving him a big smile as if to say cheer up – just as excited and nervous as he was. "… Don't forget to remove your wooly hat!" his mum joked. Eric had forgotten he was still wearing it under his top hat. He laughed and promptly pulled it off.

The band stopped and the front of house curtains started to close as guests started to pour in to take their seats.

"I'd better grab my seat before somebody else does. I'll see you in the interval darling," she said, blowing him a kiss, further adding to his embarrassment. "Believe in yourself!" She then left him, trying to squeeze her way past lots of warm sweaty bodies limbering up on the way out.

Just then one of the girl dancers handed Eric a note on a small scrap of paper. "I was told to give you this," she said, before pirouetting and jettè-ing her way back to rejoin her dance troupe. The note, scribbled in big letters, read:
Watch your back tonite, David has got something bad

planned for ya!' Well, there was only one 'David' that Eric knew, and it immediately made him start to feel ill at ease. There wasn't much room left to write anything else, except, just squeezed in at the bottom, was the word, 'Sorry!' written.

"Who gave you this note?" Eric called out to the girl, perplexed as to who it might be? Eric thought, "Whoever it was that wrote it is not very good at spelling."

"I think his name is, erm … Gary?" replied the girl.

"Gary?" Eric said to himself, trying to think of the Gary's he might know. Then it dawned on him, 'Hamburger'! "But why would he warn me about this?" wondered Eric, even more baffled. The truth is, 'Hamburger' no longer wanted to be David's friend and was sorry for all the horrible things he had done to Eric and so wanted to warn him.

"Please take your seats, Ladies and Gentlemen. The show will be starting in approximately ten minutes!" A voice was heard over the P.A system. The compère for the evening was the Deputy Head, relieved that the sound system was finally working.

The band switched off their amps and left their musical equipment where it was upstage and headed off into the stage left wings, messing about pretending to walk and groan like scary zombie's as they did. As David made his way past some of the acts waiting in the wings ready to go on stage and perform, over in the distance, above the heads of the mass of dancers, he could see someone wearing a top hat.

He quickly barged past a few of the acts to get a closer look, nearly tripping over a girl's legs who was doing the splits. Some girls gave out a scream, seeing him in his zombie makeup for the first time. And, then noticed who it was … "What's *Fartz* doing here? Oh no!" he thought to himself, very surprised to see him, having hoped that he'd put him out of action on the rugby pitch.

For a moment David just stood there motionless, giving Eric the 'Death Stare'. He then turned back, barging his way past pupils again, and angrily walked through the already open backstage exit door, which lead to outside the building. "Time to put my original plan in action and stop him entering the talent competition *once* and for *all!*" sinisterly thought David.

The three other band members of 'The Zombies' were already outside by the dilapidated bicycle sheds nearby, joking and messing about, and drinking cans of high-energy drinks; one had lit a cigarette.

"If we get caught smoking it won't matter because with all this makeup on the teachers won't recognize us!" joked one of them as he took a puff on the cigarette and passed it over to one of his mates. David went over to join them.

"That magician *Fartz* is here!" said David sounding bothered and angry.

"So, what!" said one of the band members wondering why David was so bothered.

"Yeah, don't worry about him, he's good, but were *much* better!" boasted another.

"I ain't bothered in the faintest about that *talent-less nobody!*" snapped David, jealous, and very clearly bothered by seeing Eric backstage.

"You do seem bothered?" argued one of the band members.

"I told ya, I'm *not* bothered, *now* shut it!" said David getting even more agitated.

"Anyway, I thought you said your dad was gonna have a word with one of the judges?" enquired one of them.

It's true, his dad the School Governor, had persuaded one of the judges by way of a financial incentive to give his son's band the top marks and give all the other acts poor marks. Therefore, giving 'The Zombies' an unfair advantage!

"He *has!* Now drop it *all right!* Give us a puff!"

said David reaching to take the cigarette.

"There's a *teacher,* put the cigarette out, *quick!*" said one of the lads noticing a teacher opening the stage fire exit door and triggering the security light. The teacher pocked their head outside to have a look around, wondering why the door was open?

"Hide behind these bikes!" said David as the four of them only narrowly missed getting caught. The teacher then shut the door.

"Oh great, now we're locked out!" exclaimed one of them.

By now the audience had all taken their seats, and there were even people standing at the back who had not been able to get tickets, but Eric's dad was not among them. Ingrid had turned her head around a few times looking for her ex and was a bit disappointed that he had not turned up.

Eric made his way to the wings and peeked through the stage curtain to see where his mum and Emily were sat. He could see his mum was sat a couple of rows back in the centre and Emily was sat nearer the back with her family.

"You can't stay there!" then said a slightly grumpy stage manager, indicating for Eric to move away. So, Eric went back to where he had left his magic props to find a couple of the dancers nosing around, lifting things up and trying to find out his secrets. "Come away from there!" Eric told them assertively and neatened up the props on his table again.

"Five minutes till curtains up!" announced the stage manager to the acts nervously waiting backstage. It suddenly went very quiet backstage, except for a few contestants whispering to one another and the occasional nervous giggles heard. Then after what seemed like an eternity, the stage curtains opened revealing a table on stage right with three shiny handsome trophies on it, with the biggest one in the middle for the winner.

The Deputy Head then walked out on stage smiling, carrying a radio microphone in his hand. Sat along the front row were the Head Teacher, David's dad the School Governor, and some invited guests.

"Testing, one – two. One – two. Good evening Ladies and Gentlemen, Boys and Girls and welcome to 'St. Bartholomew's Got Talent' on Friday The Thirteenth!" announced the Deputy Head in an overly theatrical voice. "Oooh! *Spooky!*" he then quipped, making light of it. The audience joined in making an 'Oooh' sound. "Now, before we start the competition, I'd like to first of all introduce to you the judges. So please will you give them a big hand as they make their way to the judge's table.

They are Mrs Sharp, who runs the local Stage School 'Twinkle Toes'; Brian Hobbs, a local businessman; and lastly, but by no means least, our Head of Dance and Drama, Miss Hopkins!"

The audience applauded as the three judges made their way to their seats at the judge's table in the centre of the hall.

"... Also, I would like you to give a warm welcome if you would please to the Deputy Mayor of Ramsgate, Bill Turner who very kindly has stepped in at the last minute for The Mayor, who I am very pleased to say is making a remarkable recovery!" then announced the compère. The audience applauded loudly as the Deputy Mayor got up, twisted around and waved his hand in the air in acknowledgement.

After clearing his throat, a couple of times, the Deputy Head then said, "Now, although we have named it 'St. Bartholomew's Got Talent'. In *our* talent competition – unlike 'Britain's Got Talent' on TV – we don't have a Mr Nasty Simon Cowell-like character or any buzzers to buzz acts off, and there are no advert breaks!" A cheer went up as he said that. "... This will be a fair and honestly judged competition, filled with great entertainment, performed for you tonight by our very talented lower school pupils!" Another even louder cheer was then heard. "… But, of course, Ladies and Gentlemen, this is a competition and there can be only one winner, and it will be up to the judges to decide who that winner will be to receive the top prize of £100.00!" The audience cheered again as the prize money was announced. "… There will also be cash prizes for the runners-up in second and third place!" Yet even more cheers applause then followed.

They certainly were a lively crowd with many of the act's families making up the audience.

"… The marking will be determined on the acts talent, presentation and entertainment value. The highest mark for each being ten," continued the Deputy Head, sweating slightly under the bright spotlight.

The Deputy Head was then handed a note from one of the teachers. "I have just been informed that a few of the acts have pulled out of the competition. So, the show will be a little bit shorter than planned – Anyway, enough of my waffling. Ladies and Gentlemen, without any further ado, it gives me great pleasure to introduce the first act on this evening – one of Seven dance troupes – please put your hands together and give a warm welcome to … *The Blasting Rockets!*'" the Deputy Head finally announced, reading the name from a slip of paper, thinking as he headed off stage, "Oh dear, did I just swear then?"

Their music started, and the audience clapped and cheered as all twelve of the female dancing troupe, six from each wing, came bounding on stage dancing the Charleston to start the show. All wearing dresses from the 1920's era – sequins flying all over the place! One dancer almost accidentally bumping into the Deputy Head as he attempted to exit the stage, causing him to start dancing embarrassingly out of her way. He was clearly not used to doing this sort of thing.

"Shh!" said the Deputy Head as he finally made it off stage, putting his forefinger to his lips to quieten down some of the other noisy entrants waiting to go on in the wings.

Eric was still backstage by his magic props practising, he dared not leave his props unattended again, in case some of the other contestants become nosy and wanted to try and discover his secrets like before.

The music ended and the audience clapped and cheered as the dancers all took a bow and then made their way off stage and into the wings. The show had got off to a good start.

The next act to be introduced, was a female singer called Sara Pilkington, wearing a lovely long flowing dress, singing 'My heart will go on' from the film 'Titanic'. She sang beautifully, and if it hadn't of been for the bow of the ship collapsing as she leaned against it singing the last note, it would have been even better! "That wasn't supposed to happen, was it? Poor girl!" A lady on the front row was heard to say. "I don't remember that happening in the film?" said another.

The Deputy Head quickly came rushing on to help her up, while a couple of stagehands hurriedly cleared away the broken pieces of stage scenery. She was all right apart from some tell, tell signs of embarrassment – running off stage with her hands covering her face sobbing. The slightly embarrassed Deputy Head then quickly introduced the next act.

"Ladies and Gentlemen, moving rapidly along. This next act doesn't need an introduction, because he can blow his own trumpet, and that's exactly what he's going to do for you now. So, would you now please put your hands together for a fine musician called *Robert* ... Wiś-ni-ew-ski!" announced the Deputy Head, reading his name from a slip paper he'd scribbled on earlier, struggling to pronounce his last name.

Meanwhile, David and his band were knocking as loud as they could on the stage door, competing with all the even louder noise inside, desperately trying to get back inside.

"Open the door! It's *freezing!*" called out David, alternating knocking at the door with blowing inside his fists to try and keep warm.

"Open the *door* and let us in!" All four of them now shouted in unison. Not just because it was cold outside, but also because someone hiding in the dark had now started throwing 'Fun Snaps', water bombs, and firing a spud gun at them. Bangs and explosions went off and could be heard to splatter against the wall and the door.

"Ouch! My *butt!"* yelled one of them, clutching his sore backside.

"It's no good, we'll have to go around to the front!" called out another.

"We'll get *told off* if we do that Einstein," said another sarcastically. Just then the door opened and one of the dancers let them in, getting the fright of her life as four zombies came rushing in groaning and moaning. Mainly from becoming cold outside and being shot at by some crazed mystery zombie hunter. The crazed mystery zombie hunter in question was 'Hamburger', who had left his mum inside and sneaked around to the back, armed to the teeth to play a prank on them, and with still the need to get his fix shooting at zombies!

The band, still wondering who the devil that was outside, mixed in with all the other entrants, and luckily for them were not spotted by any of the teachers or stage crew who were very busy trying to run the show.

"I'm *soaked!*" said David. "I bet that was one of the bullies from the year above?" he thought, feeling relieved to be inside. David left his other band members and walked in the direction of Eric who had his back turned not realising David was fast approaching.

By now a few more acts had been on and off stage performing to a very supportive audience. and the judges were busy giving each act their marks and consolidating with each other after each act had finished. "Your marks are a bit stingy?" said one of the judges to the Mr Hobbs, noticing that he had marked all the acts so far with very low marks. Mr Hobbs, who was a slippery looking character with a slightly crooked moustache, just turned his head away, ignoring the comment and promptly shielded his marks from the other judge's view.

The compère then introduced the next act who was a comedian and a welcome change from all the dancers and singers that had been on so far.

Ingrid quickly looked over her shoulder again, but there was still no sign of her ex at the back of the room, "Where could he be?" she thought to herself.

"Ladies and Gentlemen, would you now please put your hands together and welcome on stage a very funny lad who I'm sure is going to make you laugh. Give it up for *Billy Mathews!*" announced the Deputy Head. The audience clapped and cheered as the young man came bounding onstage smiling his head off. "Remember to keep it *clean* young man!" stage-whispered the Deputy Head as they passed each other on stage.

The cheeky comedian stepped up to the mic and cracked his first joke, making the audience laugh and the Deputy Head cringe. The young comedian then told one quickfire joke after another, much to the amusement and delight of the audience.

"BOO!" shouted David in Eric's left ear as he made his way around to face him. It made Eric jump, and as he moved his head away quickly to see who it was, he soon realised it was the bully David. "… What are *you* doing here then? I thought they only allowed *good* acts to enter this competition!" sniggered David looking down at little Eric, mocking him.

"I could say the same thing to you!" replied Eric bravely, not letting the bully get the better of him.

"Oi, watch it *Fartz!* Magic's boring anyway

and you don't stand a *chance* of winning against *my* band!" snarled David, slightly taken aback with Eric's comeback line, not expecting him to answer back.

"You don't *frighten* me! Why don't ya just go away and *grow* up!" said Eric standing up to the bully. Something he didn't have the confidence to do a little while back.

Angry, David then reached over and grabbed Eric's magic wand off his table and snapped it in half over his knee! But instead of Eric being upset, which David was expecting, Eric burst out laughing? He thought it was hilarious and fell about on the floor uncontrollably laughing his head off. Some of the dancers nearby were looking at Eric thinking, "The comedian's not *that* funny?"

"Why are you *laughing?*" demanded David, cross that it was him being laughed at for a change. What David hadn't realised, and which Eric had found so funny, was that he had picked up the 'Comedy Collapsible Wand', which is meant to appear broken!

The interesting thing about laughter is, it's infectious, and the sight of Eric rolled up on the floor laughing, caused others around him to join in with the laughter, not even knowing what they were laughing about. So, with that, David promptly threw the apparently broken wand down on the floor and stormed off.

Eric picked himself up along with his wand, straightened it again and put it back in place on his table. "Buying this wand was money well spent!" thought Eric, relieved that David had left and hoping that was the end of it. "That wasn't 'bad'," Eric then thought to himself, thinking about what was written on the note from 'Hamburger'. But this still wasn't what David had in store for Eric!

It was now the turn of the last act on before the interval. "Oh no, *not* more dancers!" thought the Deputy Head. So, this time he thought it wise to introduce them from off stage, especially after the near collision the last time.

Out they came, dancing to a hip-hop track, which energized the audience who clapped along to the music as the dancers, a mix of four boys and four girls strutted their stuff, body popping and break dancing all over the stage. This was the troupe that Emily's sister was in.

"Let's hear it for *'Streetz Ahead'* Ladies and Gentlemen!" The audience cheered and gave them a big round of applause, especially Emily's family of course. "… 'Streets', spelt with the letter 'Z' apparently? I must have a word with their English teacher!" quipped the Deputy Head to a few titters. "… Well, I wonder if the judges will put them *Streets Ahead* in the competition?" then joked the compère to a few groans from the audience, trying to be witty again as the dancers left the stage. "… It's now the interval Ladies and Gentlemen. Refreshments are being served at the back of the room and the second half will recommence in twenty minutes time, thank you!" The curtains closed and the house lights came on.

Ingrid looked behind her again noticing that her ex had still not arrived. Backstage there was a hub of activity as the acts appearing in the second half got changed and prepared to go on stage. Eric had already been dressed a long time ago and was raring to go.

"Will you show us some magic?" asked one of the dancers stood near to him.

"Sure!" said Eric confidently and performed an astounding trick he'd learnt from his magic book. Eric borrowed a shiny new penny from the girl and asked her to hold it tightly in her hand. By now a small crowd had gathered to witness what was going on. He told the excited girl to concentrate, and then to slowly open her hand. Upon doing so, the girl shrieked out loud, and everyone's jaws dropped! "O-M-G!" said the girl, totally amazed! Her penny was now bent! *(Find the secret to this cool trick called 'The Bent Penny' at the rear of the book!)*

CHAPTER THIRTEEN

THE TALENT COMPETITION
SECOND HALF

"The second half of the show will be starting in five minutes Ladies and Gentlemen if you would like to please take your seats!" The Deputy Head's voice was heard saying over the P.A system. Upon hearing this, the audience finished their drinks and started to sit back down again. Eric's mum was outside having a quick look around to see if her ex was there, but there was no sign of him there either. She did notice an empty can of larger on the ground near the entrance though, and it did cross through her mind, "I wonder if that was Peter's?" Ingrid quickly went back inside, and just before the second half got underway, popped through the stage door by the side of the stage, climbed up some steps and made her way past all the contestants to find her son backstage.

There he was in the same spot still surrounded by several of the other contestants admiring his magic. Eric's confidence had grown and grown!

"Shuffle the cards," Eric was heard to say. He then took back the thoroughly shuffled pack and held it behind his back. "I shall now attempt to locate the four Aces behind my back. Sight unseen – and by feel alone –"

"Break a leg love!" called out his mum quickly to her son, interrupting him for a moment. Eric acknowledged his mum with a nod, thinking, "Now even she's saying, break a leg?" and carried on performing as she went to take her seat to watch the second half.

"There's the Ace of Diamonds!" Eric announced dramatically as he brought the Ace into view from behind his back. The onlookers started to applaud. *"Wait!* I still have three more Aces to find!" Eric announced as he fumbled behind his back in search of another Ace. "Ah, *here* it is!" said Eric looking pleased with himself as he brought forth yet another Ace. Then as a finale, Eric impressively produced the last two Aces at once! The group around him applauded making too much noise. *(Learn how to perform this skilful-looking trick called 'The Easiest Four Ace Trick in the World' along with all the other tricks in 'Eric's Magic Secrets' at the rear of the book!)*

"Quieten down! Quieten down!" called out the Deputy Head who was in the wings waiting to go back on stage at any moment. Eric thought he'd better stop performing and the group dispersed. Eric wasn't on until towards the end of the show and had got a bit bored with all the waiting around.

David wasn't anywhere to be seen and even his bandmates had wondered where he was? What was he up to this time? What was he planning to do to poor Eric?

Two of the judges took their seats again; one of them was still talking with the School Governor and quickly then joined the others at the table as soon as he heard the microphone being tested.

"One – two. One – two," was heard over the P.A system. The house lights suddenly went dim; the curtains opened and out walked the Deputy Head.

"Well, Ladies and Gentlemen I hope you are all refreshed and ready to be entertained again by all our wonderful and amazing pupils?" The crowd cheered loudly answering that question.

"Well then, Ladies and Gentlemen, without any further ado, to open the second half of the show we have another street dance troupe for you – so will you please put your hands together and go wild for – *'The Streets'!"*

The music started, the audience applauded, and the Deputy Head headed quickly for the wings as the high kicking, arms flinging, hip gyrating dancers came strutting out on stage.

"It's dangerous out there! There are limbs *flying* everywhere!" said the Deputy Head to the stage manager, glad to be off stage and out of harm's way. "... Didn't they perform in the first half?" he then casually asked him, looking very confused.

"No, that was 'Streetz Ahead' – different troupe," replied the stage manager.

"Oh, they all look the *same* to me!" said the Deputy Head as he picked up his cup of half-drunk coffee, smelling as if something stronger may have been added to it?

The next act to go on after the dancers was a girl originally from Hong Kong called Victoria Wang. A virtuoso violinist who everyone thought would probably win the competition. But as she went to pick up her violin, she was suddenly heard to burst into tears and was terribly upset. The Deputy Head went over to her to see what the matter was, as did some of the pupils, who gathered around her. He didn't need to ask her because he could instantly see what had happened. Someone had purposely cut all the strings on her precious violin!

One of the female teacher's, who was also backstage helping, then came over to consul her, but the poor girl was inconsolable and wept and wept.

"I not can play now!" The Chinese girl tried to say, sobbing after every word in her broken English accent.

"Do you have spare strings?" asked the teacher trying to be of help.

"No, not enough! Someone *sabotage* my act!" replied the virtuoso still very upset and angry.

The Deputy Head left the teacher to deal with it, as he then got ready to take the dancers off stage, desperately trying to think of what to say to the audience about the crisis unfolding backstage.

"Are you ready to go on now instead?" The Deputy Head quickly asked the solo male singer. Panic clearly heard in the Deputy Head's voice.

"Errrm, y-yes s–s-sir," replied the singer with a nervous stutter, licking his dry lips and now panicking at the thought that he had to go on next and sing for the first time in front of a live audience. His hands were slightly shaking, and his legs felt like jelly – all wobbly. The poor lad was consumed with stage fright and got himself into a right tiswas!

"Are your parents in the audience?" asked the teacher to the violinist.

"Yes!" she replied very disappointed that she would not be able to take part in the competition.

"Come with me and I will escort you to them now," said the teacher.

The violinist reluctantly agreed, and clutching her tuneless violin, strings dangling and swinging about everywhere, she left with the teacher in a huff.

The dancers finished their spot and the audience cheered and applauded them as they left the stage. "Let's hear it *one* more time for The Streetz! ... Now, unfortunately, Ladies and Gentlemen, due to a technical problem. Our next act, Victoria Twang – I *mean* Wang – will not be able to perform tonight!" embarrassingly announced the Deputy Head. A big sigh of disappointment was heard in the audience. "But we have a *wonderful* singer for you now, who is going to sing a song by Robbie Williams, called 'Let me entertain you'," he continued to say, reading the singer's intro direct from his notes for the first time since he'd scribbled it down earlier. "He's a bit nervous, so please put your hands together and give a warm Bartholomew welcome to ..." There was an awkward pause. "Now where's his blooming name?" he was then accidentally overheard saying under his breath over the PA system, as his eyes desperately searched for it on his crumpled-up slip of paper. "... Oh yes, *sorry!* John Edwards!"

The audience applauded loudly as the nervous boy entered the stage.

"Oh, *God!* The violinist's parents aren't going to be very happy!" thought the Deputy Head as he quickly exited the stage even sweatier than before.

The Chinese parents of the violinist had by now been reunited with their daughter and were shocked to hear that she wouldn't be entering the competition. The father become very animated and was heard saying something in Mandarin, which translated was something like, "Is the Deputy Head taking the Mick?" They all got up in disgust with their arms around their daughter, who was still sobbing, and promptly left.

Several people turned around to see what the commotion was including Ingrid, who was also looking to see if she could spot her ex. Alas, he was not there!

"Will you *stop* keep turning around!" said an

irritated older female member of the audience, sat behind her, in a snobby voice as Ingrid turned around again for the umpteenth time.

"You mind your own *business!*" snapped back Ingrid in her strong northern, 'Don't you mess with me!' accent. The quarrel was starting to get quite heated. And at one point it looked as though a fight might break out! The music started and Ingrid turned back around to continue watching the show.

The singer slowly and anxiously reached the mic stand, somewhat dazed by all the lights, forcing a smile, still clearly very nervous. And as he opened his mouth to sing, nothing came out! He unfortunately forgot the words to the song! And then to make matters worse, when he finally remembered, he started stuttering again during the chorus, "So come on, let meee-ee entert-t-t-tain you ..." and became out of sync with the backing track music! It sounded awful! Everyone in the audience felt for the poor lad.

"It's turning out to be a disaster!" said the Deputy Head to the stage manager, peering out from the wings with both hands cupping his face. However, once the vocalist's nerves had calmed down, he soon managed to get back in time with the music and sang the rest of the song very well! The Deputy Head walked back out into the glare of the stage lights, smiling like a 'Cheshire Cat'. "… Let's hear it for *John Edwards!*"

The audience gave him an extra big round of applause and a cheer for not giving up and carrying on. And a much more confident boy exited the stage. "Well done lad!" said the compère as they passed one another, thinking to himself, "Only a few more acts left to go, thank *God!*"

The Deputy Head hadn't realised just how stressful being the master of ceremonies could be, having to get everyone's names right and deal with unforeseen technical difficulties and so on. *(Just picking up on how brave and determined the acts in the story are by entering the talent competition in the first place, despite being nervous and frightened.*

Many people from all walks of life have confidence issues and get nervous and frightened for many different reasons. And, its usually only fear that stops people from doing what they want to do in life!

So be brave and determined by not letting fear stop you doing whatever it is you want to do or being, whoever you want to be! And, don't worry about what other people may think of you! You will feel a lot better about yourself and achieve a lot more if you don't let your fears get in your way! Just go for it!)

David suddenly showed up backstage and went over to join his band.

"*Where* did *you* get to?" asked one of the band.

"Oh, I sneaked outside again to get some fresh air and a quick smoke. It's very stuffy backstage!" It was very stuffy backstage with so many bodies about, but was there another reason why David went outside?

"We thought we might have to become a trio instead tonight!" joked one of them.

"*What* and miss winning the competition. No way!" bragged David cockily.

The show progressed with yet another dance troupe, followed by a girl reciting poetry, while the judges were kept busy deliberating and writing down their marks. The compère then introduced another female singer who made her way onto the stage singing a lively up-beat number.

Eric's mum was sat, anxiously waiting in her seat for her son to come on stage next after the singer, fingers tightly crossed. Backstage, Eric started to feel the nerves again, his heart was beating even faster than the beat of the music he could hear on stage. He then remembered some advice his mum had told him, which was to count backwards from ten to one, to help focus the mind. So, this is what he did, and sure enough it did help a lot.

His top hat had been on and off his head numerous times while he waited anxiously backstage for his turn to perform. And finally, it was time to leave it on so he could use both hands to carry his table full of props over to the wings ready for a stagehand to set it on stage. All he had to do now was navigate past all the other performers still backstage, which was no easy task.

"Excuse me please!" said Eric as he tried to get past people. But as he was carrying the table, the motion caused the oversized hat to slip over his eyes as he was walking, and he couldn't see a thing. *"Sorry!* He said as he bumped into someone. Just then someone snatched his top hat off his head and started to run off with it. It was David, who had waited for this opportune moment to carry out his devious plan. David pushed open the backstage fire exit door and ran outside with Eric's hat. Eric was slightly taken aback at first, but then quickly realised who this zombie was, and promptly put his table down and bravely gave chase.

"Hey! Come back here with my hat!" Eric called out as he followed David out through the door. The music was playing loud and the Deputy Head and the stage management were too busy running the show to notice the commotion going on behind them, and the other pupils just thought it was a prank.

"I thought it was *zombies* that were supposed to do the chasing, not the other way around?" joked one of the other pupils to their friends standing nearby.

Eric needed his hat for his magic act and was desperate to get it back. The security light had automatically come on, but David was nowhere to be seen! So, Eric rushed over to have a look by the bicycle sheds and noticed his hat lying on the ground. But as soon as he reached down to pick it up, David, who'd been hiding behind a row of bikes, suddenly pounced on him from behind, forcing him to the ground. David had tricked Eric into following him!

"Get off me!" Eric screamed, powerless against the bully's sheer size and power. David looked scarier than ever with his smeared make up on. It was like a 'Zombie Horror Film' and what nightmares are made of – only this was for real! "Let me *go!*" then said Eric, angrily. "Why are you doing this?"

"Shut it! Make another sound Fartz, and I'll *punch* you hard!" threatened David through clenched teeth as he grabbed hold of a long chain from the ground nearby, which he'd planted earlier.

"I'm on stage *next*, let me *go!"* then pleaded Eric, desperately struggling to get away,

realising he was going to miss his chance to perform!

"That's what *you* think! Now *shut it* or *else!*" repeated David, trying to keep his voice down.

"*Ouch!*" screamed Eric as the nasty pitiless bully wrapped the freezing cold steel chain several times around Eric's puny wrists, pinching his skin and making them sore. David then unsympathetically grabbed poor Eric's nice tailcoat, ripping part of the silver ribbon away from the lapel as he dragged to where there was a metal roof support at the desolated far end of the bike shed.

There, David continued to tie him up – hurting Eric as he wrapped the chain tightly around his frail little body and the roof support – taking out his own frustrations on him. This was a lot tighter than Eric was used to!"

David then quickly reached into his trouser pocket, his fingers desperately fumbling around in the dark amongst lots of coins from the day's plunder and other bits and bobs in search of the padlock. His fingers finally located the padlock, and as he removed it from his pocket, a pair of sharply pointed scissors accidentally fell out onto the ground. Eric desperately cried out for help, fearing the worst. "*Shut it,* I said!" snarled the big brute again.

251

Eric suddenly recalled seeing David hanging around suspiciously by the violin just before the strings were severed. Quickly putting two and two together, he deduced that there was a strong possibility that they were the same scissors used to commit the crime! And wouldn't have been at all surprised or put it past David to do such a horrid and spiteful thing.

"Was it *you* who cut the violin strings?" asked Eric, like a detective would interrogate a suspect. "It was *you, wasn't* it!"

David didn't answer. He just carried on further tightening the chain around poor Eric in a crazed state of mind, pinching his skin again as he fastened the padlock securely through the links of the chain. It all happened very quickly and Eric's hopes of entering the talent competition were looking very bleak just like the weather, which had now turned bitterly cold.

"Now try and perform your magic tricks, *loser!*" said David, as cold as the steel chain he used to tie him up with. David rose up from his crouched over, domineering position and started to move away, his cold heart racing, feeling a massive adrenalin rush.

"I'm going to *report* you!" said Eric as he continued to struggle.

"You'd *better* not! Nobody would believe you anyway!" snarled the horribly jealous and insecure bully. He then quickly kicked the gleaming suspect scissors away from the beam of light and into the dark. No amount of make-up could hide the guilt written on his face.

"HELP! HELP!" screamed Eric out loud, starting to panic as he tried to wriggle his way out of the chain to no avail, thinking to himself, "I'm never going to escape from this chain!"

"No one's gonna hear you out here! You're wasting your breath. Don't worry I'll come and release you when I've won the competition!" boasted David as he hurriedly left Eric all alone shivering in the freezing cold, laughing as he did at his victim's predicament! It was the sort of cold one could die from if exposed to it for too long!

Eric then suddenly heard the magician's voice from the Christmas Fair in his head again, which he hadn't heard in a while, hadn't needed to, but he certainly needed all the help he could get now. As he listened, he started to pull himself together, no longer panicking and screaming, and thought to himself, "You know what, 'You're wasting your breath' is the only, and yet, best advice that bully David has ever given to me!" Eric then remembered reading one of 'Houdini's' secrets of escape was to be relaxed and calm, which made it easier to escape.

So, despite deciding not to perform a chain escape that evening, he now had no choice but to try and escape, determined not to let the bully beat him, and still enter the talent show. But this time it was going to be a real challenge, as the security light had just switched off and David had fastened the chains very tightly indeed!

David sneaked back inside the hall, still slightly out of breath and joined his bandmates again. The singer had just finished her song and the compère went on stage to take her off.

In the wings, the stage manager was starting to panic and become annoyed. *'Where's* the next act? *What's* his name? *Where's* my running order? ... *Oh yes,* 'The Amazing Fartzini', that's it! *Why* isn't he here ready to go on?" said the stage manager to one of the stagehands.

"Oh, I don't know?" replied the stagehand, and went off looking for him.

"He must have *disappeared,* sir!" quipped David, after overhearing the conversation, giggling along with his bandmates. Knowing full well where his main rival, as he saw him, was.

Moments later, the stagehand came back carrying Eric's table of magic props. "I found his table, but there is no sign of the boy!" said the stagehand to his manager, putting the table down, not knowing what to do next.

"He must have got *too* nervous and decided to leave? I see it happen all the time!" said the stage manager, and quickly scribbled something down on a slip of paper.

The Deputy Head, unaware that something was amiss, took the singer off and started to announce the next act. "Do you like magic ladies and gentlemen? ... Well, this next act is going to amaze you all! So, will you please put your hands together and welcome on stage *The Amazing —*"

Just then, before he could finish what he was saying, the stagehand came rushing on stage interrupting him, and handed him the note. The Deputy Head apologized and quickly read what was written. "... Ladies and Gentlemen the magic act that was due to go has unfortunately decided to pull out of the show – so there won't be any magic after all!" Eric's mum's heart sank upon hearing the disappointing news. "Sorry about this ladies and gentlemen – just a moment please." The Deputy Head then went over to the wings to have a quick word with stage manager, completely unaware as to the real reason why Eric was not there.

The judges all crossed out 'The Amazing Fartzini's' name as they prepared to judge the last act on the show – 'The Zombies'.

"Are the band ready?" asked the Deputy Head in a bit of a panic again.

"Yes, they are," answered the stage manager, having already quickly checked.

"Okay, tell them to get ready on stage now!" The Deputy Head then quickly rushed back on stage.

Eric had just faintly heard the compère announcing him on stage as he still struggled to escape in the dark. He managed to get one hand free and immediately reached for his mobile phone in his inner jacket pocket, but it wasn't there! Eric had left it in his school blazer pocket by mistake so he couldn't even try to ring someone for help. Time was running out fast for the would-be magician!

His mum was sat in the audience wondering why her son would have suddenly changed his mind about going on stage. She couldn't understand it. She couldn't go backstage to speak to him and find out what was the matter, because when the show was on, no one is allowed backstage. Emily and Jack were also surprised and very disappointed that Eric was not going to be performing.

The band, looking appropriately menacing as

zombies made their way over to their instruments and switched on their amps and mic, causing a horrible feedback sound. David sat down at his drum kit with a sly smirk on his face. The two guitarists, one bass and one electric, strapped on their guitars, and the lead singer stood by his mic stand ready. "Let's *blow* the roof off this place!" said the lead guitarist as he cranked up the volume on his amp.

"Well, ladies and Gentlemen, despite the show being a little bit shorter than planned, hasn't it been a *wonderful* show!" announced the Deputy Head. The audience agreed and cheered and applauded. "But we still have one more act left to go in the competition. I'd now like to introduce you to our closing act. Four very nice lads who are an asset to our school, and I believe only formed the band this term. So, Ladies and Gentlemen, without further ado, would you please put your hands together and give a warm St. Bartholomew's welcome to ... *'The Zombies'!*"

As the band started up, the slightly rosy-cheeked Deputy Head headed off into the wings for another sip of his much-needed special blend of coffee, thinking, "The band's rather loud!" and feeling relieved that his compèring duties were almost over.

The singer screeched into the microphone

some undecipherable lyrics that only the band seemed to understand, causing the first few rows to immediately place their fingers in their ears, babies and toddlers to cry, and the plastic cups of water on the judge's table to vibrate. Mindless of this, the guitarists jumped wildly up and down, thrashing their guitars and nodding their heads to the constant beat of the crazed drummer. Eric certainly had no chance of being heard now!

The unscrupulous judge in the School Governor's pocket gave David's band top marks for everything before they had even started their performance, and had marked all the other acts very low, which probably meant 'The Zombies' were sure to win!

The band, now very sweaty looking with make-up running down their faces from all that frenzied jumping around, finished the song with a loud crescendo. Immediately followed by David kicking over one of his, cymbal stands, like some famous rock star, sending it crashing to the floor! The School Governor was the first to start applauding his son's band, and began to stand up to give them a standing ovation, then quickly sat back down, after realising he was the only one.

"Aren't these seats uncomfortable!" The School Governor said to The Deputy Mayor, as if to give a reason why he got up from his seat. The front row of dignitaries smiled at the School Governor and joined in with flattering applause, more out of respect for the School Governor than for the band. The rest of the audience wasn't very impressed either and only gave a look warm response.

The Deputy Head came back on stage looking even more wobbly after finishing his drink and took the band off … "Ladies and Gentlemen please put your hands together one more time for *'The Wombles'* – *'Zombies'!* … Weren't they fantastic!" announced the Deputy Head getting confused with a 70's popular young children's TV show, slurring his words and sounding a little incoherent. "Let's hear it!"

Only the front row though seemed to agree that they were fantastic though, and after taking another bow, 'The Zombies' exited the stage confident they would win whatever.

"Well, Ladies and Gentlemen the judges will now begin to tally up their scores and we will very shortly have the results of tonight's winner!" The compère was suddenly interrupted by a commotion at the back of the room.

"Let me through, let me through please!" a voice was heard. The spotlight moved from the stage on to a slightly bedraggled figure running down the centre aisle. The figure turned around in the middle of the audience, put on his top hat and announced with gusto, "Good Evening, Ladies and Gentlemen ... My name is *The Amazing Fartzini',* and I'm a magician! Would you like to see some *magic?"*

Well, the crowd went wild, thinking it was all part of the act, and shouted, "Yes!" with excitement. Eric had managed to triumphantly escape from the chains defying the bully!

The compère was speechless for a change and the judges all looked at one another not knowing what was going on or whether he would be allowed to perform now or not?

The room was filled with anticipation and there was a momentary silence as the Deputy Head came to the front of the stage and leaned over to speak with the other organisers.

"We can't let him go on now, *surely?"* protested a biased and disgruntled School Governor.

"Let him perform!" shouted Eric's mum from the audience. Emily and Jack also then joined in, as did others. And despite the School Governor's protests the Head Teacher intervened and overruled saying, "Listen to the audience, we'll have a riot on our hands if we don't let him perform. There is still time, and besides, everybody like's a spot of magic!" The

School Governor kept silent holding his annoyance in, and begrudgingly smiled and nodded in agreement with the others.

The compère stood up and called over to the stage manager in the wings. "Bring the boys table of props on stage please!" So, one of the stagehands brought on Eric's table of magic props and set it at the front of the stage as Eric made his way up the steps and onto the stage to cheers from the crowd.

"Ladies and Gentlemen the decision has now been made to allow this young man to perform. So, without any further ado. For the second time, will you please put your hands together for *'The Amazing Fartzini'!'* The audience clapped and cheered as Eric walked across the stage and took the radio microphone out from its stand.

Backstage, David was in shock. He couldn't believe it when he heard his name announced, wondering how on earth Eric could've escaped.

"Thank you very much!" said Eric as he picked up the can of 7UP and a glass from his table. He started to pour himself a drink, and while the liquid was still pouring, Eric suddenly let go of the glass to look at his watch, and to everyone's surprise and amazement, it remained suspended in midair! "Oh, is that the time! I'd better get on with performing some magic!" The audience laughed and applauded instantaneously as Eric then re-gripped the glass and proceeded to drink from it. His mum, of course, applauded the loudest, very proud of her son. Even 'Hamburger', who was sat with his mum, was clapping hard. 'Hamburger' secretly enjoyed watching Eric perform magic.

Eric put the glass and can back down on his table and removed his top hat, placing that also on his table thinking what a lovely audience they were, pleased that his opening trick worked out just the way he'd rehearsed it.

"I went to see a magician the other day, and he performed this amazing card trick where he counted – one – two – three – four – five – six cards," said Eric as he counted them out aloud, clearly showing he had only six. "He then threw away one – two – three cards. But to everyone's amazement, when he counted the cards again, lo and behold he still had one – two – three – four – five – six cards!" Suiting the actions to the words, he tossed three cards one by one into his upturned hat and then showed to everyone's amazement that he still had six cards in his hand.

He didn't stop there either because in this incredible trick the magician repeats this sequence several times and each time Eric threw three cards into his hat and counted them again, sure enough, he still had all six cards. And each time the audience applauded louder and louder! Eric counted the cards one final time to the loudest applause yet, "One – two – three – four – five – six cards!" Eric's top hat was now filled to the brim with playing cards! What an astonishing magic trick, everybody thought. Well except David of course, who was giving him the evil eye from the stage wings.

"Thank very much Ladies and Gentlemen ... It's hot up here under these stage lights!" said Eric as he pulled a red silk hankie out of his pocket and wiped his brow. But then as he casually pulled the hankie through his hand, to the audience's amusement, the hankie changed colour from red to green! Eric pretended he hadn't noticed and just placed the hankie back into his pocket, which made it all the more amusing, getting some laughs and applause around the audience.

Eric's mum by now had given up expecting her ex to show up but thought she would have one last quick look. Well, when she turned her head around, to her pleasant surprise, there he was standing at the back amongst a crowd of people, smiling and thoroughly enjoying watching his son perform! Ingrid turned back around with a big smile on her face very pleased he did make it after all.

"For my next trick I need a volunteer!" asked Eric eagerly. People on the front row immediately shrunk down in their seats hoping it wouldn't be them being picked! Eric asked Mr Johnston – his geography teacher – sat on the front row, to assist him on stage, and reluctantly he joined Eric up on stage to a round of applause.

Eric then went on the perform the 'Change Bag' routine that he had so much enjoyed watching the magician at the Christmas Fair perform to him. After showing the bag to be completely empty, Eric asked the volunteer to wave the magic wand in the air, but as Eric handed it to him, the wand collapsed in his hand, much to the hilarity of the audience, who were now in fits of laughter!

Eric then proceeded to reach into the bag and much to the surprise and delight of the audience pulled out one handkerchief after another, all different colours, getting faster and faster as he tossed the handkerchiefs into the air. What a spectacular sight it was too! The last handkerchief he pulled out was a gigantic one. And when he opened it up, written in big letters were the words 'Applause Please'. The audience thought that was very amusing and burst into instantaneous applause! Eric thanked the volunteer as he went and sat back down again to more applause.

Eric's act was going down very well with the audience and you could see that he was enjoying himself. *(You see, when you perform, it is so important to enjoy what you are doing, because if the audience see that the entertainer is confident and relaxed and enjoying themselves, they too will be relaxed and enjoy the show!)*

"And now Ladies and Gentlemen for my last trick I need to borrow somebody's finger ring!" Announced Eric as he looked around the room for someone to loan him their ring …

After some coaxing, the Deputy Mayor reluctantly agreed to lend Eric his ring. And after struggling to remove it from one of his chubby little fingers, with the help of some saliva and a lot of twisting and pulling, he finally managed to remove it and hand it to Eric. "Here you are, young man," he said joyfully with a tinge of apprehension, slightly worried to be handing over his precious diamond-encrusted gold ring to the young and inexperienced magician. "Be careful with it – it's worth a lot of money!"

"Don't worry, I will wrap your ring in this handkerchief for safekeeping!" said Eric with a glint of mischievousness in his eye.

Eric carefully wrapped the ring inside his hankie and asked someone else on the front row a few seats away to hold it up in the air. Eric then removed an orange from his pocket and gave it to the Deputy Mayor to hold in the air also, announcing, "On the count of three the ring will disappear and reappear inside this orange!" Everyone's eyes flitted back and forth between the handkerchief and the orange not wanting to miss a thing. "Are you ready? … One … two … three!" Eric suddenly whisked away the handkerchief and the ring seemed to have just disappeared!

"Ladies and Gentlemen. Prepare to be amazed!" said the aspiring magician as he put the hankie back in his pocket, hoping that he didn't mess up his finale trick! "Now sir, would you please peel the orange …" The tension in the room was building and the room suddenly went silent, except for an odd cough or two, in anticipation of the ring ending up inside!

Eric's mum looked on slightly worried, as Eric hadn't practised this trick very much and the chance to win the competition possibly hinged on this last trick! Or so she thought?

The Deputy mayor started to peel away at the orange, bit by bit, but there was no sign of his ring? Eric looked worried. But not as much as the Deputy mayor though, who's face had dropped and began to sweat. Once all the peel was off, he broke open the orange, but the ring was not there! The school Governor looked on with glee as it looked like 'The Amazing Fartzini' was not all that amazing after all.

"Oh, I am terribly sorry, the trick must have gone wrong!" said Eric, looking disappointed and shaking his head. The Deputy Mayor didn't look very happy at all and began loosening his collar. "… But don't worry! As a way of compensation I have a gift for you!" he said, drawing everyone's attention to the large wooden gift box tied with brightly coloured ribbon on his table, which had been sitting there in full view since the beginning of his act. Everyone wondered what could be inside.

Eric quickly untied the ribbon and opened the box only to reveal another box secured with ribbon inside? The audience became more and more curious and found it highly amusing that every time they expected there to be a present inside, all there was, was yet another box.

The Deputy Mayor smiled and went along with it in good sportsmanship fashion, but all the while thinking, "I'd rather have my ring back!"

Eric had opened three boxes, each one smaller than the previous, until he finally came to the very last tiny box, which was securely locked with a padlock. Eric brought it to the front of the stage and leaned over, handing it to the Deputy Major. He then handed him a key, instructing him to open it. Surely his ring was not inside there? That *would* be amazing!

The Deputy Mayor unlocked the tiny box and slowly raised the lid and peered inside.

"… Does that gift look familiar?" announced Eric with a big smile on his face.

"There's my ring!" shrieked the Deputy Mayor all excited like he was a child once again. He couldn't believe it; he reached inside the box, picked up his ring and held it high in the air, waving it about relieved that he got his ring back, completely flabbergasted! The audience gasped and burst into rapturous applause! What an amazing feat of magic that was!

But Eric's most amazing feat of all was changing from a shy and quietly spoken boy into a now confident and popular boy! (*In case you were wondering what the wise old magician at the Christmas Fair had whispered into Eric's ear, which helped him to overcome his shyness and become more confident, it was simply: 'The real magic is within you! All you have to do is summon it up, and then you can do almost anything!' This one sentence gave Eric a lot of inner confidence and self-belief he never thought he had. In other words, we all have the capability to do amazing things, if we believe in ourselves!)*

"Thank you very much Ladies and Gentlemen!" said Eric taking a bow and smiling from ear to ear overwhelmed by how well his act had gone down with the audience.

"Ladies and Gentlemen please put your hands together for *'The Amazing Fartzini'!*" announced the Deputy Head as he came on stage to take the young magician off.

Eric walked off stage to even more applause and a lot of the audience were even chanting his name, "FARTZINI! FARTZINI! FARTZINI!" How nice it was for Eric to hear his name called out in praise for a change. Eric had given a flawless performance, but now it was up to the judge's scores! He then joined all the other acts now gathered in the wings eagerly awaiting the results as the judges counted up 'The Amazing Fartzini's' scores and determined who the winner and runners-up were.

An argument could suddenly be heard at the judge's table between the corrupt judge and the other two judges.

"Please bear with us Ladies and Gentlemen while our judges determine who will be the winner and who will be the runners-up of tonight's competition! Thank you," announced the Deputy Head, looking a bit worse for wear.

The audience all chatted amongst themselves, discussing which acts they thought should win? There was a lot of excitement in the air!

Ingrid turned around again smiling, expecting to see her ex at the back of the room still. But he was not there! He had disappeared like one of Eric's magic tricks! Ingrid was disappointed, but thought it was good that he had come along and got to see their son perform. Her mind was then distracted from such thoughts as the compère was handed three gold coloured envelopes.

Who could be the winner? Did Eric score enough marks to win or be a runner-up, despite one of the judges cheating?

You could feel the tension in the room. The room then went silent in anticipation as the compère spoke into the mic.

"Well, Ladies and Gentlemen hasn't it been a wonderful evening of entertainment! Have you enjoyed yourselves?"

"Yes!" shouted the audience.

"The judges have all said how difficult it's been to judge with so many good acts in the competition! Well, it's now time to announce the results!" announced the Deputy Head. "Will you please put your hands together and welcome on stage the Deputy Mayor of

Ramsgate, who will hand out the prizes."

The Deputy Mayor then made his way up onto the stage and over to the trophy table.

"Okay, Ladies and Gentlemen," said the compère, "in third place, winning a cash prize of £25.00 is ..." The compère paused from speaking as he ripped opened the appropriate envelope and removed the card to see whose name was on it? "... The comedian *Billy Mathews!*"

The audience applauded and cheered as the ever-smiling young comedian made his way out onto the stage, squeezing past all the other anxious contestants backstage.

"Congratulations!" said the Deputy Mayor as he shook the chuffed boy's hand and handed over his trophy and prize money. "If you just go and stand over there to one side please."

"In second place are ..." the compère announced as he fumbled to remove the card from the envelope, suddenly burping out loud, much to the disgust of the Head Teacher and a few of the other dignitaries on the front row. "... *'Streetz Ahead'!*"

The audience applauded and cheered loudly once again, especially Emily's family, as the stage suddenly filled with outstretched limbs of noisy and excited dancers. It was a fantastic display of dancing they had put on for everyone!

Eric's mum by now was even more nervous than ever, sat on the edge of her seat, anxiously waiting in anticipation to hear if her son's name was going to be called out?

Backstage the cocky and arrogant David was standing with his bandmates bragging again. "We've got this in the bag boys!" said David, positive they were going to win.

"And now Ladies and Gentlemen, it gives me great pleasure to now announce the winner of 'St. Bartholomew's Got Talent', who will receive this wonderful trophy and a cash prize of £100.00!" enthusiastically announced the Deputy Head as he gestured towards the shiny trophy being held up by the Deputy Mayor.

Who could the winner be? Eric and all the other acts waited nervously backstage hoping it would be their name called out. The Deputy Head then opened the final golden envelope and slowly removed the card with the name of the winner on it, pausing to build up the suspense like on the TV, before making the announcement. "... Ladies and Gentlemen the winner of 'St. Bartholomew's Got Talent' is ... *The Amazing Fartzini'!*"

THE END.

273

ERIC'S MAGIC TRICK SECRETS

Written by Shane Robinson
&
Illustrated by Alexandra Stone

CONTENTS

The French Drop

To make coins disappear as Eric did in the story, you need to learn the basic sleight of hand technique called 'The French Drop' or 'Le Tourniquet'. This is a very useful and versatile technique to vanish a coin or coins or in fact any small object!

Hold a coin/s in your palm up left or right hand by its edges between your first and second finger and thumb, displaying the coin to the spectators (Figure 1. Exposed magician's view).

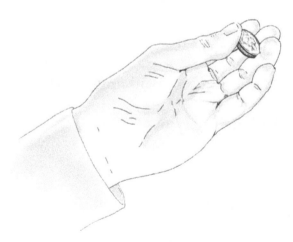

Figure 1

Let's assume you are holding the coin in your left hand. Your right-hand approaches the coin palm downwards as if to take the coin but as the fingers shield the coin momentarily from the spectator's view, your left thumb releases its grip on the coin to allow the coin to drop, hence the name, and fall into a finger palm position out of sight (Figure 2. Exposed magician's view).

Figure 2

In a continuous action, you pretend to grip the coin between your right fingertips and thumb and carry the coin away as if it has the coin, closing this hand into a loose fist and holding it up slightly, looking at your hand to draw attention to it. It is important that your left-hand remains motionless as the coin is seemingly taken away so the spectators will see an empty space where the coin was seen moments before, which adds to the deceptiveness. You then casually relax your left hand and let it fall naturally to your side or relax on the table if you're sat down.

Now to vanish the coin, act as if you are squeezing the coin or crumpling the coin and then slowly open your right-hand palm upwards to show the coin or coins have vanished.

If you wish to vanish a few coins, just have the coins stacked together, and as you pretend to take them, release all of them into your finger-palm position and the sound they make as they drop will be the same as if you did take them in your right hand.

You could practise this technique in front of the mirror to check you are performing it correctly. The important thing is to make sure it looks natural and if you believe you really have taken the coin/s then so will the spectators!

Now in the story, Eric showed both his hands empty, which really fooled David and 'Hamburger', and one effective way to do this is as follows:

Being at school Eric wore a blazer, but you

could wear any type clothing, as long as it has side pockets. Once you have performed the 'French Drop' and supposedly taken the coin/s away into your right hand, focus all your attention upon it, while your left arm moves across your body to pull up your right sleeve from underneath using your left thumb and forefinger to apparently show that there is nothing up your sleeve. However, in the action of doing so, craftily, as your left hand nears the opening of your right-side jacket pocket, you secretly allow the coin/s to drop unseen into the pocket. Sneaky huh! You then move your left hand away allowing it to relax and vanish the coin/s as above. You can now show both hands empty!

If vanishing more than one coin, to cover the noise of the coins falling into your pocket, shake your right-hand fist as if shaking the coins. Also, make sure there is nothing in your pocket that will cause a noise when you drop the coin into it! And, you could place a handkerchief for example into the pocket to help keep it open, which will make it easier for you.

If you are sat down at a table, another good way to completely vanish the coins is to perform the 'French Drop', and as you draw attention to your right hand, casually relax your left hand, bringing it to a position overhanging the tables edge and drop the coin/s onto your lap (known as 'Lapping'). Then after a few moments, bring your left hand above your right hand and make a magic gesture, and open your right hand to show the coin/s has vanished and both your hands are seen empty!

If you wish to reproduce the coin/s, keep the coin/s hidden in your left-hand finger-palm position and after you have performed the vanish, simply reach into the air or behind someone's ear for instance, and pretend to make the coin/s re-appear by pushing the coin/s up into view at the fingertips. This way you won't have to dispose of the coin/s hidden in your left hand.

The Transformation of One Object to Another

It's very useful to learn how to switch one small object for another, and in the next incredible trick I am going to teach you how to do just that. This technique is called the 'Bobo Switch'.

To switch one coin for another, for example, hide the coin to be switched in your right-hand finger-palm position. Using the right hand first two fingers and thumb, with the back of your hand towards the spectators the whole time, pick up a different value coin and display it casually at your fingertips, being careful to keep the palmed coin hidden from view (Figure 1. Exposed magician's view).

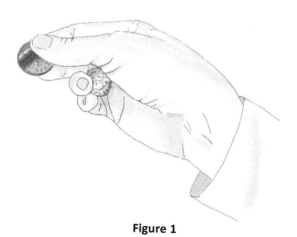

Figure 1

Now toss the coin over into your waiting palm up left hand, which catches it and immediately closes over the coin as it does. Repeat this action once or twice (this is to condition the audience into accepting this action as being normal, so they are not suspicious when you do make the switch).

Now without looking at your hands, the third time you go to throw the coin over to your left hand, two things happen at once. You maintain your grip on the visible coin, and instead of throwing this coin, you release the finger palmed coin instead, by extending your right fingers slightly, which immediately cover and hide the switched coin from view (Figure 2. Exposed magician's view).

Figure 2

As before, you should immediately close your left hand over what is assumed to be the same coin to conceal it as your right hand casually drops to your side, finger palming the coin.

Then blow on your hand, or however else you wish to present it, and open your left hand to reveal the object has been transformed! When the switch is performed properly the spectators will not notice a switch has been made! It should be performed casually on the offbeat.

You can use this switch with a number of small items. For instance, as well as changing one coin into a completely different coin, you could magically change a coin into a sweetie or a chocolate! Magicians often use this switch when they need to switch a regular coin for a gimmick or gaff coin.

The Bent Penny

Well, now that you have learnt how to switch one coin for another, you are ready to learn this next amazing, trick! In the story, Eric amazed his fellow contestants backstage by causing a penny to become bent! This is one of those tricks where it is the presentation that makes all the difference between people thinking they have witnessed a mere trick or a miracle. Really!

To perform this trick, you will first need to make a bend in the penny. And, unless you're Superman, the easiest way to do this is to use two pairs of pliers and, gripping the coin between them on either side, bend the coin so it becomes sufficiently bent. It is more impressive if the coin is seen to be only slightly bent, rather than if it has a huge bend in it, as it will be less believable.

I also recommend bending several pennies at a time, because in this trick it is more impressive if you borrow a penny from someone, and at the end of the trick return the coin to them in a bent condition so that they have a memento of your performance. Of course, you can use other coins as well if you wish.

Before you are about to perform the trick, finger palm the bent penny in your right hand.

Ask to borrow a penny from the audience, making sure it resembles the one that you have hidden, and display it at your right-hand fingertips. Now look around as if looking for a suitable volunteer, saying, "For this experiment I need a volunteer," and while you are talking, casually toss the borrowed penny into your palm up left hand, immediately closing it as you catch it. Repeat this once or twice, finally making 'The Bobo Switch' as explained in the previous trick.

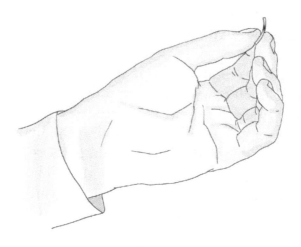

Figure 1

Now, because in this trick you are using two coins of the same value and it is only a slight bend in the coin, you can even push the coin part way up above your left fingertips to display

287

it as if it's still the same coin – making sure the bend is hidden from view (Figure 1. Exposed magician's view).

To make it even more convincing you can even toss the coin up into the air and catch it without the bend in the coin being noticed. Remember, the audience at this stage don't know what you are about to do, so they are not looking out for it!

Then ask the spectator to hold out their right hand, and here, if you wish, you could demonstrate how you want them to hold their hand by turning your right-hand palm upwards, still hiding their switched coin behind your curled fingers, while you casually show your right hand is empty. This is very deceptive and being a small coin it's easy to hide.

Now place the bent coin onto the palm of the spectator's right hand, keeping the bend in the coin concealed, and tell them to close their hand over the coin, saying something like, "So no one can get at it!" Once this is done, as a precaution, ask them to turn their hand over palm down so they are less likely to open it prematurely.

The spectator won't be able to tell that the penny is bent when it is in their closed hand since the coin is only slightly bent! Dispose of the switched coin in your right hand by casually dropping it into your pocket when it is convenient.

Now the work is done, it's now all just down to presentation and how you sell it, so to speak! Turn the conversation around to the paranormal and how some people can somehow harness unseen energy and bend metal with their minds! Ask the spectator to grip the penny tightly, and after a little while say to the spectator, "Focus on the coin," and then ask them if they can feel the metal getting warmer. More times than not they will confirm this to be true as it will naturally get warmer in their hand anyway. Now say to them, "Try to use the power of your mind to cause the penny to change its molecular structure," or words to that effect.

To finish ask the spectator to very slowly open their hand! Then be prepared for the screams as people freak out just like the spectator in the story!

You could even have the spectator apparently initial their coin with a permanent marker pen. But in reality, once the switch is made, you have them initial the bent penny while you are still holding it at your left fingertips, hiding the bend. The coin is then placed into their hand and you continue performing it as above. The effect is even stronger this way!

Congratulate the spectator on their amazing paranormal ability and leave them with the bent penny to remind them of this incredible experience.

The Rubber Spoon

To perform this fun and surprising trick, all you require is a metal teaspoon. It is an ideal trick to prank your friends and family when you are out and about in a café or restaurant, or having a cup of tea around someone's house, as Eric did at his mum's friend's house.

Figure 1

To start off with, pick up a teaspoon in your right hand and hold it vertically by the handle in a loose fist with the bowl visibly facing outwards towards the spectators, fingers wrapped around the front of the spoon with the pad of the thumb pressed against the top rear part of the handle, and place the tip of the bowl against the table, or your knee (Figure 1. Audience view).

Now bring your left hand over and clasp the right hand, covering the right-hand fingers and the tip of the spoon handle completely, as if to get a good grip on the spoon with both hands to seemingly use more force to bend the spoon against the table. As the left-hand covers and conceals the right-hand fingers, the right little finger tip repositions itself behind the lower part of the handle to act as a hinge. This is where your acting skill now comes in because you need to make it look as if you are bending the spoon against the table.

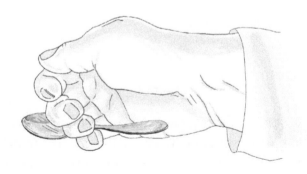

Figure 2

To do this, tilt your hands forwards only (using some shoulder movement as if you are forcibly bending the spoon in half), while at the same time allowing the handle of the spoon to secretly lower behind your hands. The illusion of the spoon being bent is perfect! You could say as Eric did in the story that the cutlery must be made of rubber, which the audience will find amusing (Figure 2. Exposed magician's view).

Once you have seemingly bent the spoon in half, keeping the state of the spoon concealed from the spectators, cover the spoon with both hands, with one hand overlapping the other, wiggle the fingers as if making a magical gesture and then after a moment remove your hands to reveal the spoon is fully restored! Much to the relief of whoever's spoon, it belongs to! Practise this fun trick to make it look realistic!

The Centre Tear

This trick will make people think you have genuine mind-reading powers! In the story, Eric asked a spectator to write down the name of a famous person on a small piece of paper and fold the paper into quarters to hide what they had written. The paper was even torn up to destroy the evidence. Yet Eric was able to read the spectators mind and name the person she was thinking of correctly.

Figure 1

To perform this astonishing feat, all you need is a slip of blank paper approximately eight centimetres square and a pen or pencil. Ask a spectator to think of the name of a famous person, dead or alive, as Eric did in the story (or something else if you prefer.) While they are doing that, draw a large circle approximately four centimetres in diameter in the centre of the paper (Figure 1). Then tell them, "So as to get a strong mental image of the person in your head, please write down the name of the person in the circle."

Turn your head away from them as they do this. Then instruct them to fold the paper in half and then into quarters, explaining, so you can't see what they've written. When they have done that, take the folded paper back from them with your right hand, holding the paper so that the folded edges are at the top right-hand corner (this is the area that contains the name and the reason why you ask the spectator to write in the circle). Now without hesitation and without looking at your hands, rip the paper in half vertically placing the left-hand piece in front of the right. Then in a continuing action turn the pieces horizontally to the right and tear the paper once again into quarters, placing the left-hand pieces in front of the right again. So as to seemingly destroy any evidence of what they wrote.

You are now going to secretly steal away the piece of paper closest to you, which has the information written on it, so you can secretly read what it says. As soon as you finish ripping up the paper, take the pieces from your right-hand fingertips with your left-hand fingertips, but as you do, your right thumb simply pulls back the top folded piece and retains it in the right hand, secretly hidden behind the fingers (Figure 2. Exposed magician's view).

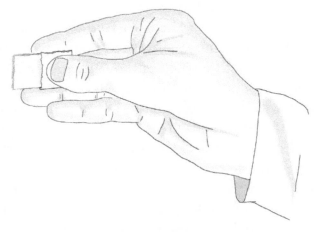

Figure 2

Now discard the pieces of paper in the left hand as you ask the spectator to concentrate on the name of the person they are thinking of, while you attempt to read their mind. (When you tear up the paper and discard the pieces, act as if it's not important.)

All you need to do now is to secretly open the piece of paper and read the information written on it. There are several ways you could do this. For instance, when you place the pen back into your pocket, you could unfold the paper using one hand by pushing the folds open with your thumb, assisted by your fingers. Then bring your hand out of your pocket with the slip of paper concealed in your hand and casually glance at what is written – perhaps as you place your hand to your forehead to concentrate. Then after a dramatic pause, astonish everyone by naming the thought of person.

Another way is to pick up a small pad, which you tore the piece of paper from initially, and use this as cover to secretly unfold the paper and note what is written, all the while pretending to read their mind, writing down one letter at a time in your attempt to divine the name of the person they are thinking of before finally naming it correctly!

If you are sat down at a table, you can secretly open the folded paper on your lap and glance at it.

Lucky Thirteen

This is a strange and spooky card trick, which I created myself, and it's very baffling and surprising! Thirteen is supposed to be an unlucky number, but in this trick, it proves to be lucky.

A card is selected and returned to the pack and despite the pack being cut thirteen times, when the pack is spread, all the cards are now shown to be in their various suits and in numerical order, except for the chosen card which is the only card out of position! But as if that wasn't strange enough – the chosen card is seen to be in the thirteenth position from the top of the pack! Now that's lucky!

To perform this very surprising trick, first you need to secretly arrange the cards in their numerical and suit order: Ace through to King (the Ace being at the top of the face down pack). Just remember, which King is on the bottom or 'Face' of the pack. Herein lies the main secret to the trick.

At the start of the performance if you can give the pack a 'False Shuffle' retaining the complete order, then do so, but it is not necessary. Spread the cards out face down between both hands and ask a spectator to remove a card, remember it and show it to some other spectators.

Then, when they are looking at the card and showing it around to others, secretly count twelve cards from the top of the pack and separate your hands at this point to have the chosen card returned to the top of your left-hand cards. Place the cards in your right hand on top so their card will be in the thirteenth position from the top of the pack unbeknownst to the audience. I turn my head away as the card is returned to suggest everything is fair.

Now once the card is returned, square the pack and set it down on the table in front of the spectator. Talk about superstitions and that the number thirteen is supposed to be an unlucky number, but for you, it's a lucky number! Then offer to show them.

Tell the spectator who chose the card that you would like them to cut the pack and complete the cut twelve times to mix up the pack and lose their card, but you will cut the pack the thirteenth time. Count out loud as each cut is made (Figure 1).

Once the pack has been cut twelve times, you remind them you will cut the pack one final time making it thirteen cuts in all. Now to return the cards to their original order and re-position the chosen card thirteenth from the top, is simply cut the pack, bringing the original bottom King back to the face of the pack, because no matter how many times the cards are cut it will not affect the original order otherwise.

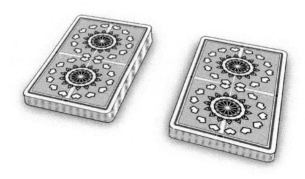

Figure 1

The easiest way to do this is to casually pick up the pack and spread the faces of the cards towards you and simply cut the original bottom King to the face of the pack, counting, 'Thirteen'. (There are several other ways to achieve this, including using a 'Short Card', a 'Thick Card' and the method I use, which is using a 'Crimp Card'. For a brief explanation refer to the 'Glossary'.)

Now say to the audience that despite the cards being well and truly mixed up, you will attempt to locate their card. The pack is then spread face up on the table showing to everyone's surprise and amazement the cards are now in numerical and suit order, except the chosen card which is the only card not! Act as if the trick is over and then after a short pause, also point out that their chosen card is located at the thirteenth position in the pack! Proving that the number thirteen is a lucky number for you!

As regards to secretly counting twelve cards from the top of the pack; a much easier way is to put a light pencil dot on the back of the Queen at the diagonally opposite left-hand corners, so that you can easily spot the position of the twelfth card in the spread.

It is recommended to have two matching packs, with one of them pre-arranged as above and hidden in your pocket, while you first perform one or two card tricks with the other pack, clearly showing the cards are mixed up. You casually put the pack away in the same pocket as the pre-arranged pack and perform some other type of trick. Then as you offer to show them one more card trick you simply bring out your pre-arranged pack and perform 'Lucky Thirteen'. It is an ideal card trick to finish on!

The Linking Rubber Bands

This amazing trick was invented by a magician called Dan Harlan. It is the trick which Eric performed for his friend Jack on their way to school, where two rubber bands link and unlink most mysteriously.

For this little miracle, all you need are two thin rubber bands, ideally size # 19 (1.6mm thickness and 88.9mm diameter) or a similar size. Whatever size is best for your size hands.

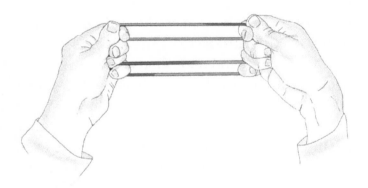

Figure 1

Start the trick by having the bands examined, and once that's been done, take them back and display one of the bands stretched out between the curled forefingers of both hands and the other band by both your curled little fingers

(Figure 1. Magician's view).

Now in order to make it look like the band's link and unlike with one another, first you must secretly swap the two middle strands around one another.

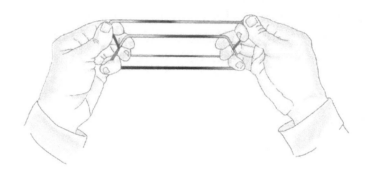

Figure 2

To do this, after holding the bands up at chest height, displaying the bands to the spectators, casually lower your hands to about waist height, relaxing the tension on the bands. And then as you are talking to them and taking attention away from the bands, casually swap the two middle strands around using the thumb of the right hand and the middle finger of the left hand, wrapping the bands completely around one another, and insert the middle and third fingers of both hands inside the loop thus formed and re-grip the bands by curling these fingers inwards (Figure 2. Exposed magician's view).

To cover this action, you could casually stretch the bands back and forth a couple of times – the bigger motion concealing the smaller motion. Now bring you're your hands up to chest height again and stretch the bands out. To the audience, the bands will look exactly the same as they were before.

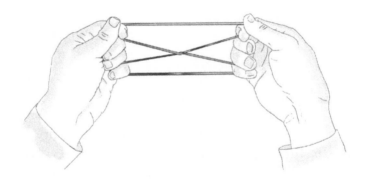

Figure 3

Now ask a spectator stood opposite you, to gently rub the two middle strands together using their thumb and forefinger. As if to illustrate, extend the middle and third fingers of your left hand and rub the bands together yourself for a moment; afterwards curling your two fingers inwards again. After they have rubbed the bands a couple more times, ask them to slowly remove their fingers. And to everyone's astonishment it will look like the two bands have linked together (Figure 3. Magician's view). Say something like, Look, you must have magic powers! You've caused the two bands to link together! That's incredible!"

Now using your right thumb, you can push the top band's bottom strand away from you, while at the same time, twisting your wrists back and forth in opposite directions to really emphasise this!

Now all you have to do is ask the spectator to rub the two middle strands together again, and as they do, simply move your middle and third fingers of the right hand unnoticeably and release the bands. When the spectator removes their fingers, to everyone's further surprise, the bands will now be separated. A miracle! No wonder Jack was so amazed!

The Glass Through the Table

This trick is a showstopper and well worth the time and effort to practise and learn it. A classic trick that always gets gasps. It is also an excellent lesson in misdirection. A solid glass penetrates through a solid table! This is the same trick, remember, that Eric performed in the school dining room, and is ideal to perform anywhere you are sat down at a table having a meal or a drink.

All you require is a small glass or plastic tumbler, a paper napkin, and a coin. Oh yes, and a table of course! You need to be seated with your legs together, allowing some space between you and the tables' edge. With the props already on the table, tell your audience that you are going to cause the coin to penetrate through the solid table. To emphasis this, you could tap the edge of the coin against the table as you say it.

Place the coin on the table, about thirty centimetres in front of you and turn the glass upside down, placing it over the coin. Now you need to create a mold for the glass using the paper napkin. So, unfold the paper napkin and place the centre of the napkin over the top of the glass so the glass will be completely concealed and mold the napkin to the shape of the glass (Figure 1).

If you were to remove the paper mold or shell, it should still maintain its shape and look as though there is still a glass under it – which is a large part of the secret.

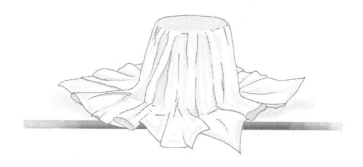

Figure 1

To give a logical reason why you cover the glass with the napkin, you could say, "I shall cover the glass with the napkin so as to shield the secret in mystery!" Now lift the napkin covered glass up with your right hand, fingers wrapped around the front side with your thumb at the rear, to show the coin is still on the table. While at the same time, place your left hand under the table as if to catch the coin. Now say, "On the count of three, the coin will pass through the solid table! One – two – three!" As you say "three", lift the glass and bring it back towards you, resting it at the edge of the table with the rim of the glass just below the table, acting surprised and a little disappointed to see the coin is still there. What you are doing is conditioning the audience into thinking this is a natural and innocent action, because the next time you do that you are going to secretly release the glass out of its paper shell so it falls onto your lap unbeknownst to the audience (Figure 2. Exposed magician's view).

Figure 2

Say something like, "Oh dear! The coin should have gone through the table. Let me try that again." Suiting the actions to the words, proceed to cover the coin with the glass again, making a noise as you set it back down onto the table. Count to three and once again lift the glass, bringing it back to the table's edge as before. But this time, secretly drop the glass out of the paper shell and onto your lap, drawing all the attention to the coin on the table as you do, saying to the audience, "The trick seems to have gone wrong? One last try!" Make the audience believe it really has gone wrong. This is misdirection.

Now without hesitation, move your right hand forwards to cover the coin with the paper shell (which the audience still believe has the glass under it); while at the same time, placing your left hand under the table to pick up the glass and bring it directly under the same spot as the coin. Now as you set the paper shell down over the coin, simultaneously knock the glass against the underside of the table, so it will sound like it's still above it. This helps to make it very convincing and deceptive!

For the finale, say something like, "I have confidence it will work this time. On the count of three! Three!" Just say the word "three" and suddenly slam the palm of your hand down on top of the paper shell and squash it flat against the table. The audience will be taken by complete surprise and it will really look as if the glass has penetrated right through the table. Pause for just a moment, to let this amazing effect sink in with your audience. And acting as if you caught the glass, bring your left hand out from under the table, triumphantly showing the glass, and finish by saying, "Oh look! The glass has gone through the table instead!"

I recommend that you use a good quality paper napkin or serviette (the stiffer the better) when performing this trick, so the napkin holds the shape of the glass better. When holding the napkin covered glass, to help maintain the shape after the glass is removed, I clip a small part of the paper near the top edge of the glass between my first and second fingers.

After witnessing this trick, just like those who watched Eric perform it, your audience will be amazed too!

The Ubiquitous Pen Caps

Here is a fun thing to do with a pen cap, which can be combined with the previous trick. The magician removes the cap from the pen and places it in his pocket only to discover that the cap has re-appeared in his other hand! Once again, the pen cap is removed, but this time another pen cap appears! This is repeated, again and again, as pen caps keep appearing much to the surprise and annoyance of the magician!

To perform this trick, all you require is a pen and a matching pen cap. Have the pen with the cap on it along with the matching cap in your left-side jacket or trouser pocket.

To start the trick: reach into your left side pocket and pick up the pen with its cap uppermost, along with the matching cap, secretly hiding it from view as you bring your hand out from your pocket (Figure 1. Exposed magician's view).

Now casually remove the cap from the top of the pen with your right hand and place it in your right-side pocket. While you are doing this, casually toss the pen down onto the table or give it to someone to hold for a moment, secretly retaining the matching cap in your loosely closed left-hand finger-palm position.

Figure 1

Now two things should happen at the same time: you casually look at your left hand and act surprised as you open your hand displaying the pen cap to have suddenly re-appeared, while you only pretend to leave the cap in your right-hand pocket, but retain it secretly hidden in the 'Thumb-palm' position as you remove your hand from your pocket. (To 'Thumb-palm' the cap, simply close your hand into a fist and clip the top of the cap between your thumb and the upper side of your palm). The 'Thumb-palm' allows you to open your fingers slightly giving your hand the appearance of being empty and will help facilitate this trick. The focus should be on your left hand

You are now going to perform what is

known in magic as the 'Put and Take Move'. Basically, as you remove the cap from your left-hand fingertips, you replace it with the cap secretly held in the thumb-palm position (Figure 2. Exposed magician's view).

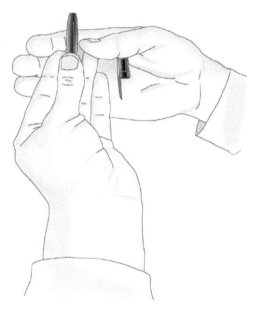

Figure 2

Now, after the cap is shown to have initially re-appeared in your left hand: display the cap, now holding it between your left first and second fingertips and thumb, with the top of the cap pointing upwards. The right hand, with the other cap hidden in the thumb-palm position, approaches the left hand, and the right first and second fingers and thumb, grip the cap in the left hand towards the bottom and removes it in an upwards direction; while at the same time, deposits the thumb palmed cap in exactly the same position where the other cap previously was a moment ago. (Phew! That was a lot to explain!) It should look like, as you remove the cap from the left hand, another one magically appears in its place!

As you remove the cap from your left hand and place it in your right-hand pocket pretend at first not to notice another cap has appeared. But as before you re-palm the cap into the thumb-palm position and remove your hand from your pocket. Now noticing another cap has appeared, I usually do a 'double take' and act surprised and slightly perplexed. And then continue repeating these antics several more times, using the same method explained above: placing the caps in my pocket as they keep appearing, and doing it faster and faster as I act more and more flustered and bothered, as if it is out of my control. It looks very comical to see!

For a surprise ending, put a pen cap of a different colour or an entirely different small object in your right- hand pocket, and the last time your right hand goes to your pocket to supposedly deposit the cap, this time actually release it and thumb-palm the other object and make that appear instead!

Also, because you are only using two pen caps: another climax would be to show all the pens caps you have produced have vanished! This way you get an additional effect. Simply pretend to place the last cap in your pocket, but secretly retain it, and then show your pocket empty.

As already mentioned, this trick makes an ideal lead in to 'The Vanishing Pen Cap Trick'. You decide that the only way to stop the pen caps from keep appearing – is to make them disappear!

The Cut and Restored Earphones

This trick is sure to get your audience's attention! Although this trick is very easy to do, if you perform it well, you'll get great reactions just like Eric did in the story. If you remember, he borrowed someone's earphones and cut the wire in half. Then miraculously restored it – much to the boy's relief. It is a fun trick that certainly has the shock factor!

Lots of people wear earphones to listen to their favourite music, so there should always be someone about with earphones you could borrow to perform this amazing quick trick. The trick is most effective if you borrow someone else's earphones and act as if it hadn't been planned, so it appears that you decided to perform it on the spur of the moment. It's also best to perform the trick briskly, so once you've cut the wires and show them to be apparently separate, you immediately restore them! This way, you have the shock value – but also, you don't give the audience the chance to think about how it was done!

To perform this trick, you are going to need a supply of the same type of black or white wire used with most earphones sets, plus a pair of scissors.

To prepare: cut off a length of approximately twelve centimetres and simply fold the wire in half. (We will refer to this wire as the gimmick.) Place the wire and the scissors together in your left-side pocket, ensuring that when you remove them, the loop will be uppermost. And you will now be set to create a stir!

Ask someone if you may borrow their earphones for a moment to demonstrate a magic trick. As they are handed to you, take them in your right hand by the centre, so the wire is doubled in half, forming a loop. Then remove the scissors along with the gimmick and place the scissors somewhere convenient for a moment, keeping the gimmick secretly hidden from view in your loosely closed left hand. Now what you are going to do is switch the loop in your right hand for the gimmick loop in your left hand.

Very casually, whilst looking at the spectator/s and talking to them, simply bring the right hand loop up from under the left hand, leaving it behind in the lower part of your left hand, holding it in place with your left little and third fingertips, and in a continuous movement and without hesitation, pick up the gimmick loop and bring it up into view about three or four centimetres above the left hand (Figure 1. Exposed magician's view).

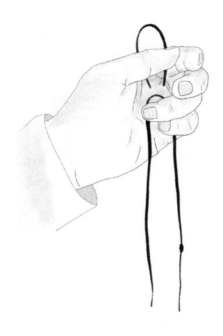

Figure 1

Now pick up the scissors with your right hand and cut the gimmick loop in half. To the audience, it should look like you just transferred the earphones wire from one hand to the other so you can pick up the scissors with your right hand to cut the wire. The audience will be shocked that you have cut the wire in half, so play it up a little.

Put the scissors away and hold up your hand to clearly display the cut wire. Now after only a convince the spectators it is a real knot. Then hold the tie outstretched between both hands, displaying the knot in the centre (Figure 2. Magician's view).

Now to make the knot disappear, simply blow on it for effect, and at the same time pull the tie sharply in opposite directions so the knot will instantly come apart! A real surprise!

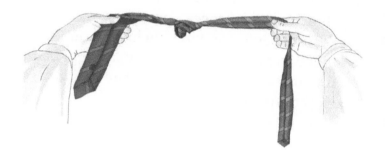

Figure 2

When you are forming the knot, it is important to act like you are genuinely tying a knot (if you believe it, so will your spectator's), and not to draw too much attention to it by looking at it!

Here's a fun and very magically trick you can also perform once you have learnt how to make a false knot. Secretly hide a rubber bouncing ball, a sweetie, or even a Yo-Yo, for instance, in your right hand. You can still form the false knot using your right thumb and first finger with your other fingers curled inwards, secretly hiding the object.

Now when you have formed the false knot, hold up the tie by one end in your left hand and display it hanging down. Your right hand grips the knot and pulls sharply downwards and away, causing the knot to dissolve, and you immediately throw the ball on the ground, catching it as it bounces upwards. Or a Yo-Yo could suddenly unwind, which you then continue to play with. Or open your right hand to reveal a sweetie or a chocolate for a very magical transformation effect!

The Magic Spell

To accomplish this excellent card trick, we once again call on our friend 'The Key Card' to help. It's a fun trick to perform, and apart from a pack of cards, the only other thing you require is the ability to spell.

A card is selected and lost in the pack. The magician first looks through the pack in an attempt to find the chosen card to no avail. So, decides to spell out the name of the card, dealing one card face down onto the table for each letter spelt. When the last letter is spelt and the card is turned face upwards, it proves to be the very selected card! Amazing!

As with the above trick, once the pack is shuffled, memorise the bottom card of the pack, which is your 'Key Card'. Then have a card selected and memorised by the spectator/s and returned to the top of the face-down pack. Ask the spectator to then cut the pack and complete the cut. At this point, if you wish, you could have the pack cut several times or 'Overhand Shuffled'.

Now spread the cards between your hands, with the faces of the cards towards you, one card at a time from your left hand over to your right hand using your left thumb, as if attempting to find the chosen card. Act as if you are having trouble finding it. Once you reach your 'Key Card', remember the name of the card below it, which will be the chosen one. And without hesitation, continue spreading cards singly while silently spelling one card for each letter, starting with the chosen one. For instance, if the chosen card is, let's say, the 'Four of Clubs', you will push eleven cards in total over to your right-hand group of cards. At this point, act as if you cannot find the card and are about to give up, and casually separate your hands, placing all the cards in your left hand underneath those cards in your right hand. So essentially, you have cut the pack and secretly brought the number of cards needed to spell out the chosen card to the top of the pack.

Now to magically reveal the spectator's chosen card, all you need to do is spell it out! Ask the spectator to name their card. Here I say, "We don't need a magic spell to find your card. All we need to do is spell it out!" Then hand the spectator the pack and ask them along with all the other spectators to slowly spell out the name of the card and to deal one card for each letter face downwards onto the table in a pile. When the last card is dealt, ask the spectator to turn the card over, which will reveal their chosen card! Hurrah!

If you wish – as by way of a demonstration –

you could first spell to a seemingly random card yourself, turning over the last card dealt to reveal that card.

To do this: once the chosen card is spelt out in the spread, simply continue spreading the cards while spelling out the name of the very next card until that card is spelt out also. Then, as before, cut all the cards above the last card spelt to the bottom of the pack, so the random card will be ready to be spelt out first and revealed before the spectator's chosen card.

If you run out of cards at the top of the pack when you are spelling, simply continue spreading and spelling one card at a time from the bottom or face of the pack.

Number 18

This is a very clever mathematical trick that will astound your audience based on 'The Nine Principle'. It is a 'Force', which can be used in many ways. Here is my favourite way of using it. The good news is that it's a self-working trick and you don't have to do any arithmetic — the spectator does! All you've got to do is instruct them.

The only set up required is to write down on a slip of paper the value of the 18th card from the top of a pack of cards. Fold the paper into quarters; this will be your prediction. You will also require a pen and a pad or a piece of paper.

Place the pack of cards in full view on the table and hand someone your prediction to look after for safe keeping. Then ask someone to write down any three-digit number containing all different numbers. Next to reverse the numbers so they have a new number, and to write whichever is the smaller number under the larger number so they can subtract one three-digit number from the other. When they have done the subtraction, they will have another new number.

Now lastly, tell them to add these individual numbers together so that they arrive at a random smaller number.

Take the pencil back from the spectator and insert the pencil tip into the opening of the secret channel. And then push or tap the pencil downwards sharply, pretending to pierce a hole right through the centre of the banknote.

For dramatic effect and to build up the suspense, hold the pencil in place with your left fingers for a moment or two before pushing the pencil seemingly through the banknote (Figure 2. Exposed magician's view). It's a great illusion! And from the front it really looks like you've pierced a hole right through their banknote and damaged it!

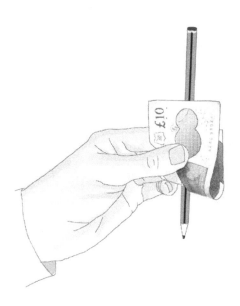

Figure 2

To restore the banknote: pull the pencil all the way through, and then holding the ends of the folded banknote in each hand, bring it up to your mouth, blow on it for effect, and then quickly snap it open showing that it is now fully restored! Rustle the banknote to remove any telltale creases in it before you hand it back. A miracle!

You could also present this as a penetration type trick showing that solid can indeed pass through solid!

The Mobile Magician

This trick is appropriately named because it uses a mobile phone, and you can perform it anywhere – as most of us carry one around with us wherever we go! This is the surprising and delightful magic trick Eric performed to Emily on their way home from school, where he produced a 3D chocolate for her from just a photo on his phone! But once you know the secret, you will also be able to produce a whole manner of different things!

Firstly, you will need to set your phone up as follows: using your camera phone, take a photo of the object you wish to produce on a black background. For instance, a chocolate as in the story, making sure the photo appears the same size as the 3D object you will produce. And, take another photo of just the black background, and store these two photos side by side in your photo gallery, with the photo of the object positioned to the right.

Before the performance, secrete the object you wish to produce inside your left-side pocket next to your phone. When ready to perform, reach into your pocket and remove your phone along with the object, hidden underneath it (Figure 1. Exposed magician's view).

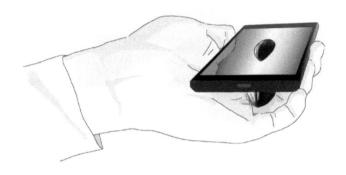

Figure 1

If you wish to produce a chocolate, for instance, say to someone, "Would you like a chocolate?" Then reach into your right-side pocket and act as if you are searching for it. But bring your empty hand out saying, "Nothing there!" Now, without looking at it, transfer the phone and the chocolate over to your right hand, keeping it hidden under the phone, holding it in place with your fingers. Now having freed your left hand, go in search of the chocolate in a left-side pocket.

Acting a little disappointed, bring out your hand, showing it empty as well, saying, "Sorry, I thought I had one left?" In the process of searching for the chocolate, both hands have been casually shown empty, which is very

Figure 2

When you are attempting to escape, drum up as much acting ability as possible, and to help build the suspense, firstly, wriggle about and act as if you are struggling to escape. This is known as showmanship and adds to the drama, so when you do finally escape, it will look more impressive!

GLOSSARY

Listed in Alphabetical order below are the explanations for magic terms used throughout the book, which you will find useful.

Bottom of the Pack: The 'Bottom of the Pack' refers to the bottom or lowermost most playing card of the face-down pack. Also called 'The Face of the Pack'.

Card Control: A method for secretly controlling the spectator's chosen card – either usually to the top or bottom of the pack.

Card Force: A method used to 'Force' a playing card to be chosen, which the magician has predetermined unbeknownst to the audience.

Complete Cut: The action of cutting or dividing the pack and then placing the bottom packet directly on top of the other. Thus, completing the cut.

Crimp Card: A playing card which has secretly been crimped or bent slightly in one corner to enable the magician to easily locate it using the thumb and cut the desired card to the top or bottom of the pack.

Ditch: A method of secretly disposing of an object, such as a 'Gimmick', using 'Misdirection' and ditching it in your pocket, on your lap, or up your sleeve.

Escape: An 'Escape' is a feat demonstrated by escaping from a restraint such as chains, like Eric performed in the story, handcuffs or a straitjacket, made famous by 'Harry Houdini'.

Face-down: The face or value of a playing card is orientated facing downwards so the back design is uppermost.

Face-up: The face or value of a playing card is orientated facing upwards.

Fake Transfer: The name given to any 'Sleight' where the magician simulates transferring any small object from one hand to the other, secretly retaining it in the hand, such as 'The French Drop' for instance.

Finger-palm: A small object, such as a coin or ball, is secretly hidden in the hand at base of the curled fingers.

Gimmick: A 'Gimmick' refers to an object that has been modified or altered so as to facilitate performing a certain trick.

Key Card: A 'Key Card' is a playing card which is secretly noted by the magician and usually placed directly above or below the spectator's chosen card after a 'Complete Cut', enabling the magician to locate the chosen card by searching for their 'Key Card'.

Lapping: The term used for secretly disposing of items, using 'Misdirection', onto your lap when sat down at a table.

Mind Reading: The act of seemingly reading a person's mind and then naming what it is they are thinking of.

Misdirection: A technique used by magicians to draw or distract the audiences' attention away from the method used to accomplish the trick.

Overhand Shuffle: This is one of the most common ways to shuffle cards. The pack is held in the right hand by the narrow ends, edgeways over the palm up left hand, and the left thumb pulls away small clumps of cards until the whole pack is exhausted, and the same procedure is repeated again. Hence the name 'Over Hand Shuffle'.

Pack of Cards: Also known as a 'Deck of Cards'. It consists of fifty-two playing cards comprising of four suits, which are Hearts, Clubs, Diamonds and Spades with thirteen cards in each suite, Ace through to King, plus a Joker.

Pre-arranged Pack: A pack of cards which is secretly set up in a certain order to facilitate the trick before the performance commences.

Prediction: When something is predicted or foretold before it happens. The magician or mentalist normally makes a prediction by writing down the name of something on a slip of paper before it is chosen or named.

Riffle: The action of flicking the cards quickly by bending the pack and releasing cards one by one. Usually performed in a 'Riffle Shuffle' or as a way to have a card selected.

Routine: A number of short tricks or 'Effects'

strung together in a certain order to make a longer flowing 'Routine'.

Secret Preparation: The 'Secret Preparation' refers to preparing and setting up the tricks you are going to perform in secret prior to your performance, so as not to reveal the secrets or how the tricks are done to your audience.

Self-working Tricks: Tricks classified as easy-to-perform and not requiring sleight of hand; often mathematical or which use a pre-arranged pack of cards.

Short Card: A playing card which has been shaved along one of its narrow ends or at one corner, enabling the magician to easily locate it by riffling the pack upwards using the thumb.

Shuffle: The pack of cards is 'shuffled' or mixed using of an 'Overhand Shuffle' for instance.

Sleight of Hand: A term used to describe secret manipulation techniques known as 'Sleights' or 'Moves' using your hands to accomplish the magic tricks.

Steal: A method used to secretly remove or

'steal' an object from view using 'Misdirection'.

Switch: A sleight of hand technique used for secretly exchanging one object for another, such as 'The Bobo Switch'.

The French Drop: A sleight of hand technique, also known as 'Le Tourniquet', used for vanishing a coin/s or other small objects, where you pretend to remove the coin from one hand to the other but secretly retain it hidden in the hand.

Thick Card: Two playing cards glued together to enable the magician to easily locate the 'Thick Card' by riffling the pack upwards with the thumb.

Thumb-palm: A small object, such as a coin, is secretly hidden by clipping it between the thumb and the upper side of the palm.

Top of the Pack: The 'Top of the Pack' refers to the top or uppermost playing card of the face-down pack.

SOME WORDS OF WISDOM TO ASPIRING WIZARDS

Remember to practise and rehearse your magic enough times so that you have a polished performance. And in no time at all, you will be amazing and entertaining people just like Eric in the story, and you'll find the more you do it, the better you will become, and your confidence will grow and grow!

I recommend not trying to learn too many magic tricks at once! It is better to concentrate on learning one magic trick at a time until you have mastered it before moving on to learn another.

Also, it is better to learn a fewer number of magic tricks and perform them very well rather than try and learn a lot of magic tricks and not perform them very well! There is a well-known story about the famous nineteenth-century English magician named David Devant, who when approached by a young novice magician boasting about the vast number of magic tricks he knew, replied that he knew eight tricks. Meaning, of course, that he knew how to perform those eight tricks very well!

When choosing magic tricks to perform, pick the ones which are not only amazing and impactful but also have good entertainment value. The magic tricks I teach in this book I have chosen for that very reason!

A lot of the methods taught can be applied to other magic tricks as well, and in some of the magic tricks, you can vary the items used. For instance, instead of vanishing a coin, it could be a small ball. Or instead of floating a bread roll, it could be an apple. So, try to be creative and original when performing magic!

Sometimes when you are performing magic, you will make mistakes and be criticised; it happens to even the best magicians, so don't worry! You mustn't let that put you off because you are still only learning your craft remember. The same applies to anything in life: it is by making mistakes that one learns and improves. So don't be too hard on yourself. It's okay to fail as long as you keep trying – you're not a failure until you give up! And remember to pat yourself on the back and praise yourself whenever you are successful or achieve something.

Also, criticism can be positive and helpful, so

do listen to peoples comments and remarks, but be astute about what advice you decide to take. Not everybody is right, so don't take it too much to heart.

Never let anyone put you off from performing magic, or anything else, by telling you that you won't be able to do it, or that you're no good at it! Be positive and determined, believe in yourself and go for it! At least then you can say to yourself that you tried!

It is important not to perform just magic tricks: make your performance engaging and entertaining! Otherwise, it will appear as if you are merely presenting puzzles — and puzzles can become boring after a while. The real moment of magic is when your spectators unknowingly suspend their disbelief, even for just a moment, and become transfixed in wonderment! The most incredible magic happens in the spectators' heads, so fill their heads with wonder! Creating wonderment is what all good magicians strive for during their performance.

And remember — as the wise old magician in the story referred to as he whispered into Eric's ear — It's YOU that's the magic and not the tricks! Sometimes it's good to remind yourself of this when you are about to perform. So, sparkle and make YOUR magic come to life!

Sell yourself to your audience. There is an old show business saying, which goes along the lines of: "If the audience likes you as a person, then they will like what you do!" How very true! By being likeable, it will get you much closer to where you want to be in life, whatever it is you want to be!

The most important thing is to have fun and enjoy what you are performing. If you enjoy yourself, then so will your audience!

Here are some golden rules to remember when performing magic. Stick with these, and you won't go far wrong!

Always practise and rehearse enough times so that you can give a well-polished performance!

Don't make your magic tricks and routines too long and drawn out, as this would be boring for your audience and they will lose interest. It is better to make the performance of each trick short and direct and easy to follow to have maximum impact!

Choose to perform the type of magic tricks which are amazing, impactful and have

entertainment value.

Learn fewer magic tricks and perform them very well, rather than try and learn lots of magic tricks not perform them very well!

Never repeat the same magic trick immediately afterwards to the same audience, as it won't be a surprise and they will know what to expect, and then they might figure out how you do it!

Never reveal the secrets to your magic tricks to non-magicians, as the wonderment will be lost and it will spoil it for your audience. And what's more, you will get a lot less credit for being a good magician!

Make your performances captivating and entertaining, creating a sense of wonder so your audiences will enjoy themselves and therefore be more likely to remember you!

Be yourself, so you come across as relaxed, and remember to smile and use eye contact! Connect with your audience by communicating with them on their level, so you find common ground – and by taking an interest in them, they in return will take an interest in you! By doing this, it will give the impression that you are friendly and confident and will set the audience's mind's at ease from the start, so they will be ready to enjoy your performance.

There is a right time and place to perform magic! In other words, don't perform to people who clearly don't want to watch magic, or to people who are being awkward or not very kind. Pick your moment. That way you will get a much better and positive response!

Never admit when a magic trick has gone wrong! Carry on regardless, performing a different magic trick if necessary, or make a joke out of it. Remember, the audience doesn't know what to expect!

When performing magic tricks, never show you are annoyed or get upset when things don't go to plan. Keep your chin up and carry on being positive and likeable! As it is far better for people to say about you, "They messed that magic trick up, but wasn't they a nice person!" Rather than, "They messed that magic trick up, and I didn't like that person and never want to watch them perform again!"

'Don't hide your light under a bush'! Be a 'Show off', but don't be a 'Cocky Show off'! In other words, perform your magic tricks often and promote yourself, but don't be arrogant or conceited with it. No one likes somebody who's like that! When you perform, always be courteous and polite.

And most importantly, have FUN!

LASTLY

Thank you very much for buying my book. I hope you have enjoyed reading the story and learning the magic tricks and the advice given. The main thing to do now is to get yourself out socializing, making new friends and entertaining people by performing the amazing magic tricks you have learnt!

I thoroughly recommend taking up magic as a hobby, as performing magic is not only very enjoyable but can also be extremely rewarding. And if you would like to purchase any of the marketed magic tricks mentioned in this book and much more, please visit my online magic shop www.zanesmagicshop.com

The reason I included an illustration of a locked door – apart from being a fun and imaginative way of unlocking the door to discover the magic trick secrets within – was to serve as a metaphor for opening doors in life and creating opportunity! Performing magic has created a lot of opportunity for me, which I may not have had otherwise.

I have found performing magic to be a great leveller and a means by which to find common ground and communicate and make connections with all types of people from all walks of life and backgrounds. And communication and getting on with people is so important in life, especially a happy life!

When it came to choosing a name for the protagonist and the title of my book, I wanted to choose one that was comical to make a point. One of the main messages I wanted to get across in writing this book is not to let a funny or unusual name, or the way you look or talk, or even a disability be an obstacle or a reason for you not to try and pursue what you desire out of life. But instead, believe in yourself and go straight on ahead and do it! You will feel a lot happier and much more content for it. Remember Mr Potter's favourite Latin Saying: "Carpe diem!"

Also, happiness makes you feel more confident – so do things that make you happy!

And lastly, be a child and don't grow up too quickly, as you're only a child once remember! (I have never grown up!) So, allow yourself to imagine and dream and have fun being amazing!

I wish you all the very best on your magical journey of life!

Shane Robinson (aka Zane)

DON'T MISS!

'THE AMAZING FARTZINI II:
The magical adventures of a
boy wizard continue ...'

OUT NOW!

ACKNOWLEDGEMENTS

I would very much like to thank all the magicians who dreamt up the marvellous magic tricks taught within these pages.

I would also very much like to thank Alexandra Stone for creating wondrous illustrations from my imagination.

And, I would like to especially thank my beloved wife Angela and our son Jake for being so supportive of me in my endeavour to write this book.

ABOUT THE AUTHOR

Shane Robinson was born in Ramsgate, Kent, in 1963. Before he became a children's author, he was a professional magician. His interest in magic started at the young age of ten. He went on to become a successful magician under the stage name of 'Zane', performing at top venues around the world, including cruise liners such as the world-famous QE2.

And, as well as still performing magic, he is also the owner of an internet magic shop called 'www.zanesmagicshop.com' and is the creator of several marketed magic trick products sold around the world.

He has also appeared in two critically acclaimed movies performing magic: 'Funny Bones' and 'Magicians'.

He regularly trades at various public events in the UK, demonstrating and selling beginners magic tricks and books to delighted children, and inspiring the next generation of magicians.

He is very happily married to Angela, and they have a son named Jake.

Lightning Source UK Ltd.
Milton Keynes UK
UKHW011515190721
387405UK00001B/189

9 781916 235618